The Blue Spong *and the* Flight from Mediocrity

THE BLUE SPONG
AND THE FLIGHT FROM
MEDIOCRITY

St. Sukie
de la
Croix

Lethe Press
Maple Shade, New Jersey

Published by Lethe Press
118 Heritage Ave, Maple Shade, NJ 08052
lethepressbooks.com

ISBN: 978-1-59021-608-8

Cover and interior design
by Inkspiral Design

For Ian,

my candle in the darkness.

"All greatness of character is dependent on individuality. The man who has no other existence than that which he partakes in common with all around him, will never have any other than an existence of mediocrity."

— James F. Cooper

ONE

Charlotte, Maude and Amelia, the Clam Sisters, reclined in their family rowing boat on the River of Life. None of them bothered to touch the oars resting in their rowlocks. Each wore a big hat but none of them dared to adorn their brims with ribbons and feathers. The sisters wanted nothing more than to drift along dragging their fingers in the water. Or envy the mediocre sun, which was neither too bright, too yellow, too demanding of the sky. The river's temperature was that of old syrup. Now and then, one of the Clams would open her mouth, as if to say something, but then would lapse into silence, because who wanted to disrupt an ideally lazy, mundane afternoon?

A SPIRITED MAN stood atop a soapbox. The handlebar mustache almost covered the cigar he chewed and smoked. Amelia Clam, youngest of the Clam sisters, had to admit to herself that even more noxious than the tobacco stink was the man's claims: Kaiser Wilhelm II was born *sans* testicles! Although the Emperor of Germany had abdicated some years earlier and was now exiled in the Netherlands, enjoying the protection of Queen Wilhelmina, the disgraced militarist with an eagle atop his helmet remained a tender topic with German émigrés in Chicago.

"By having no testicles, do you mean he lacks courage?" A heckler in the crowd laughed. Others joined in.

"I mean that he is the grandson of Queen Victoria and none of her children, or their children, have testicles."

"Not even her daughters?"

The man moved the cigar to the other side of his mouth. "No. Not even them."

The assembled rabble laughed uproariously, some of the men bent double, coughing and spitting out wads of masticated tobacco. The war had poked a stick into the hornets' nest of Chicago's socialist and anarchist immigrants and the stinging buzz still reverberated in 1924.

A short burly man elbowed his way through the crowd. "This is outrageous!" The man sounded British. "Our Royals have the same number of…testicles as any other family, no more, no less, but equal in quantity." Now at the front of the excited crowd, he challenged the mustached soapboxer face to face. "And you, my good man, are a cad, and a bounder." The Brit lifted his cane and succeeded in toppling the mustached man in one try. He jumped down from the soapbox and roundhoused the Englishman in the face.

The boisterous crowd gave their first honest cheer at this display of fisticuffs.

Anxious, Amelia held her bag close to her chest and waited until the scuffle and rowdy difference of opinion over the status of Kaiser Wilhelm II's clappers subsided. She then pushed her way through the bugs at Bughouse Square, Chicago's open-air free-speech forum. A trip to Eckert's Bakery could be treacherous on a Saturday afternoon in this part of town, but Amelia was unable to resist the allure of the shop's Angel Divinity Cake, chocolate nougat, and Florida Teas with Lady Baltimore icing. Navigating the blustery straits of political, religious, and other eccentric fads and notions preached by the soapboxers in Bughouse Square was a small price to pay for blissful moments alone in her bedroom with Eckert's cakes and Indian tea.

Her stomach had been her guide since earlier that day, when she had walked to Tebbetts & Garland on Michigan Avenue, where she purchased a brick of Emmentaler cheese. "It's moist with a nutty flavor," the T&G assistant sang the phrase from under a marcel wave. Her silver round eyeglasses with celluloid rims made it look as if an owl, trapped by daytime, had given up the woods to sell fine dairy products.

"Thank you, madam."

The assistant handed Amelia the package. "It's moist with a nutty flavor." Those grand eyes blinked.

Now Amelia was heading home, Palourde Parlor at 35 E. Chestnut Street, a four-story Victorian house where she lived with her sisters Maude and Charlotte. Every local knew the Three Clam Sisters.

"It's moist with a nutty flavor." The shop girl's lilting voice echoed in Amelia's head as she turned the corner onto Chestnut. "It's moist with a nutty flavor."

The wrought-iron curlicue gates at number 35 stood tall and

imposing, installed two years after the house was built in 1895 by her late father, Richard Clam, once a lawyer at the prominent firm of Clam, Hardwick, Jefferson, and Sideswipe. Amelia pushed open the gate, stepped through, then made sure to lock it behind her. The once salubrious neighborhood known as Tower Town had changed in recent years: radicals, artists, writers and men described in the dailies as "temperamental theatrical types" seemed insistent on ousting the residents of the nearby houses.

Amelia carried the cakes downstairs to the kitchen and neatly stacked them onto a porcelain shelf in the Bohn Syphon refrigerator. Aside from the three Clam sisters, Palourde Parlor was home to a housekeeper, the parlor and chamber maids, a cook, and the only resident with testicles, a chauffeur and odd-job man who, for modesty's sake, resided in the coach house above the garage. Much later, the Clam Sisters would laugh over this unnecessary precaution, as Edward Henderson favored not the fairer but the hairier sex.

The house once boasted additional waitstaff—a butler, lady's maid, and valet—but they had taken employment elsewhere after the death of Richard Clam and his wife Sarah, some five years past, when the couple had walked to the station at Wellington Avenue, held hands, kissed, then jumped onto the rails when the next train arrived.

The incident was never spoken of at Palourde Parlor. Perhaps it hadn't happened at all, and the Clams had boarded the train at the elevated platform and followed it on towards San Francisco, perhaps to its final stop in the Pacific Ocean.

In his last will and testament, Richard Clam left strict instructions to his three daughters: as mother did not want any man to touch her girls (Maude being twenty-three, Charlotte twenty-one, and Amelia nineteen at the time of the tragedy), none were allowed to court, and since father feared for his daughters' moral character, none were allowed to leave Palourde Parlor. So too, the staff must remain employed for the next five years. Those five years were nearly up and the remaining servants embraced routine. All the occupants led lives of stupefying mediocrity.

At least the death of Richard and Sarah Clam had thawed the icy Victorian formality between Upstairs and Downstairs; not enough to melt and co-mingle, but the Clam Sisters remained benevolent masters, the staff below stairs salaried slaves.

However, 1924 heralded a new world: a device to evenly slice bread could be found in stores; women could cast a ballot; the Great War, the last war of kings, destroyed half of Europe, transforming the French landscape from rural peasantry into fields of graves with Veteran's Day red poppies. As the war ebbed, the rabble, inspired by Karl Marx, toppled the Russia monarchy. Isms were *au courant*: Cubism, Surrealism, Anarchism and Marxism. Not that the staff at Palourde Parlor were Bolsheviks, far from it. A mind-numbing mediocrity stifled any thoughts of revolution in that household. They owned two of the bread slicers but no one had used either device to date.

Bianka Morietta, a petite Italian woman in her early twenties, stood in the doorway to the scullery cradling a basket overflowing with carrots and onions. "Miss Amelia, I didn't hear you come in."

Amelia offered a brief smile to the cook. "I just arrived. I bought Emmentaler cheese from Tebbetts & Garland. I'm reliably informed it's moist with a nutty flavor. Perhaps we could try some tomorrow afternoon, if you could make some Owendaw bread to go with it." Amelia glanced in the direction of one of the bread slicers. She eyed it as she had the morning's demagogue. "The Eckert's cakes in the refrigerator are mine, and our little secret, don't tell the sisters, or they'll disappear."

She waited for Bianka to take the package. "And where are Maude and Charlotte?"

"Miss Maude is at the beach painting, Edward is with her, and Miss Charlotte is on the roof tending her plants. Tonight I believe you will be dining out."

Amelia nodded. "Yes, the piano recital." Amelia bit her lip, a sign she was trying to calculate time. "Eight o'clock at the Fine Arts building, though I can't say I'm looking forward to it." She sighed. "Afterwards there will be a light buffet supper. If Maude comes in, do tell her I'm on the roof with Charlotte."

A LAW ON the books cited bathing-suit skirts could be no higher than four inches above a woman's knee. And that no man was allowed to enhance his groin with any padding amounting to more than the same four inches. Both edicts were largely ignored by the younger folk who went to Oak Street Beach, which teemed with people sunning themselves, reading books, wading in Lake Michigan's cool waters. Maude tsked at the few brave souls who ventured further out and swam. She was unaware of the canoodling, even kissing, between young men and women—or perhaps she chose not to witness any display of declining morals, as she sat on a folding chair with a canvas propped up on an easel. She rather doodled and dabbed and daubed the majestic Drake Hotel, a venue from which Station WGN broadcast a nightly program of musical entertainments. Radio was Maude's passion. The previous evening the soprano Rosemary Hughes had sung a song called "Absent," written by John

W. Metcalf and Catherine Young Glen. Maude knew every detail, full to the brim with minutiae: Metcalf penned the lyrics only after three weeks abstaining from any hot beverage; Glen refused to wear jewelry on her left side, the tall trees referenced in the song would certainly be *Sequoia sempervirens*. The paintbrush hovered over her blue sky and Maude sang quietly to herself. *Sometimes, between love's shadows on the grass. The little waves of truant sunlight pass. My eyes grow dim with tenderness the while. Thinking I see you—thinking I see you smile.* Maude smiled and added paint to her sky. Leaning back, she studied the painting and sighed, relaxed. She wore a light green flowered crêpe-de-Chine silk frock with white lace on the sleeves. Her hat, made of tan georgette, had a high-draped crown trimmed with goose feathers and a wide brim. On the grass nearby lay a hazelnut-colored parasol, folded and unneeded. Maude bathed in the dappled shadows cast by a towering catalpa tree.

Nearby, Edward Henderson rested in the driver's seat of the Clams' Kelly-green Buick convertible (bought at the Gambill Motor Company on Michigan Avenue—the salesman had worn a vest the exact same shade as the automobile). The sunlight reflected off the highly polished chrome. Edward serviced the convertible often: Every day he ran a cloth over the metal, he drained the radiator, flushed out the circulating system, also the crankcase. He inspected the oil in the transmission and rear axle, adjusted the tappets, filled the battery with distilled water and tightened the nuts and bolts. He knew he looked dapper in a pair of white flannel trousers, a white shirt with the sleeves rolled up, a lightweight slipover sweater and, on his feet, a pair of white bucks. Staycom pomade slicked back his sandy-colored hair. A sister brand waxed the tips of his fine mustache. Edward was thirty years of age, older than the three Clam sisters. To be hired as chauffeur to a family like the Clams was a step up from his humble beginnings. His father butchered hog in the South Side slaughterhouses. His mother had died trying to force another Henderson into the world. No painting beachfront hotels for them. Just a life of smeared pig's blood. Poverty. Edward closed his eyes, reflected on his lucky escape from the bloodbath, the fortuitous encounter with Richard Clam in the Huron Street Turkish bathhouse ten years earlier. Edward had surprised Richard with his depth—not of character but of ass (Richard often began any seduction with an apology about the length and girth of his cock). Richard then took Edward under his wing, employed him as a chauffeur, and behind locked doors sought new depths as sweetly as any straying spouse could. A copy of *The Jungle* by Upton Sinclair lay on the seat next to Edward, the story of a Lithuanian immigrant, his family, and his conversion to socialism. Edward had yet to finish the book.

Maude cooed to him, "Edward, I think it's time we went home. But we need to prop this painting up in the back seat of the car somehow. It's not dry yet. Let's leave it for a few minutes. It'll dry somewhat."

"It's a very short drive, miss."

Maude sat next to Edward on the front seat of the Buick, the painting of the Drake Hotel propped up on the back seat, protected from the dust and street debris by a tented sheet.

Edward and Maude hid behind sunglasses, currently in vogue among Hollywood movie stars. Edward had every issue of *Movie Weekly* stacked on a bookshelf in his rooms in the coach house. He was an inveterate moviegoer. Edward and Maude shared a passion for Gloria Swanson. They both agreed her last film, *Scandal,* an adaptation of the Alfred Sutro play *The Laughing Lady,* was disappointing. Swanson played Marjorie Colbert, a woman who, neglected by her husband, befriends Harrison Peters, who mistakes her interest for love. The unlikely plot ends in an ugly divorce. Of Swanson's performance, Maude wondered, "Why was she dressed like the Queen of Sheba?" Edward critiqued, "And what was that gesture she kept making with her hand? It was like a cavewoman." They had seen enough Gloria Swanson movies to feel confident in their opinions.

Along East Walton Place, she removed her hat to feel the wind in her hair. She imagined it might blow away the cobwebs accumulated from twenty-eight years of life. It didn't. After her parents' death, a pall of sadness had settled upon Palourde Parlor and still hung there. What they needed was a storm to disperse the atmosphere of the house. Or perhaps a tornado could lift it from its moorings and drop it somewhere more refreshing.

Edward dropped Maude outside the front gates of Palourde Parlor, then drove to the alley at the back and parked in the garage. He debated whether or not to bother bringing the book inside. His evenings, since Mr. Clam's passing, were decidedly dull.

On the roof of the house, Charlotte tended her vines, the warm breeze gently caressing her bare arms. Her private rooms were on the fourth floor, a double-door in her bedroom opening onto a rooftop garden of potted plants and cages of canaries, nightingales, and one garrulous parrot. There was also a marble birdbath, several urns, a couch hammock, a small table and a "Dorothy Perkins" arbor.

Amelia brought a hand up to shield her sight from the sun,

then sank into a rocker, woven in nut-brown willow cane, with upholstered seat and cushions in orange cretonne, and watched as Charlotte watered her tomato plants.

"Are you looking forward to the recital tonight?" Charlotte picked a dead leaf and crumbled it between her fingertips.

"No. I'm only going because it's a friend of Maude's."

"We're of like minds. We don't even know this woman. What's her name?"

"Minnie Fish-Griffin. I'll wager it'll be Schumann, Brahms and Chopin again, I just know it will." Amelia shivered. "Did you feel that?"

Charlotte looked at her sister and felt nothing. Nothing at all. "I have no idea what you mean."

"I was certain the air had a deathly chill."

"Here, under this sun?" Charlotte offered the briefest of laughs. She thought her sister needed to stop being so childish.

"I think someone is walking on my grave," Amelia said.

Their parents' funeral had been closed caskets, of course.

TWO

Palourde Parlor imprisoned the Clam sisters with dark drapes and morbid photographs of the dead lined up on sideboards. This Victorian edifice was protected from the outside world by two tall fences, one of wrought iron, the other of wealth, tradition and privilege, all the more impenetrable. Yet its inhabitants told themselves the house was a refuge, one idyllic in its promise of life free from financial woes.

A small world it might have been, but Palourde Parlor was not without secrets scribbled onto scraps of air and hidden away in closets, only to be read by spiders and ghosts. The "suicide pact" of Richard and Sarah Clam could have resulted from distress: the shared, extreme anxiety caused by the betrayal of high society's mores by the former's intimacy with the chauffeur or the latter's passion for the type of love espoused by Leopold von Sacher-Masoch through the attentions of strapping railroad workers brought to the bedroom. Or perhaps guilt: the husband avoiding the bruises his wife covered up with make-up, the wife's difficulty falling asleep in the massive bed by herself. Not all questions have simple answers. However, the three Clam daughters led lives of utter banality. Perhaps if they had been privy to their parents' secret lives mediocrity would be as foreign to them as Swahili. But the Clam sisters wallowed in their mediocrity like hippopotami in a Nile mud-bank.

At the Sunday morning breakfast table, the previous evening's piano recital was discussed. The parlor maid Celie poured coffee, while the Clam sisters helped themselves to scrambled eggs and bacon, oatmeal with fresh cream, toast, hard rolls, and honey waffles with maple sap.

"I thought the recital was inspiring." Maude buttered a slice of toast. "I particularly liked Minnie's rendition of Robert Schumann's *Lied italienischer Marinari*...the Italian Mariners' song."

"I think the clumsy cow rather pounded it to death." In Charlotte's larder of responses, subtlety was on the top shelf, out of reach.

Maude's knife slipped and slick crumbs tumbled onto the white tablecloth. "Pounded it?!"

Charlotte nodded. "Like Jack Dempsey with his gloves off. What do you think, Amelia?"

"I think it doesn't really matter. She is Maude's friend, so let *her* decide whether the pianist excelled or not. I don't see how our opinions matter one way or the other."

Secretly, Amelia agreed with Charlotte. Minnie Fish-Griffin had beaten Schumann's music to a bloody pulp before dumping the composition's lifeless body in a shallow grave, to be dug up by pariah dogs and torn apart by crows. But the chairs at the event had been comfortable.

After breakfast the Clams retired to their rooms and dressed for church, meeting in the hallway an hour later. Sarah, their mother, had been Roman Catholic, devoted to Lenten fasts and an eager reader of the several rare pamphlets detailing the Scourging at the Pillar. Her suicide was all the more shameful because of her faith. At least Father was Presbyterian.. The family Bible was kept in the study, carelessly wedged in a bookcase between a book of poetry by some hoary fellow from New Jersey and a first edition of *Nana*. The Bible showed no signs of being rifled through in a pious frenzy, though the parlor maid, while dusting, once found a photograph of a nude Mediterranean boy she assumed to be a young King David.

As the day offered a lovely sunny morning, the Clam sisters strolled the few blocks to Holy Name Cathedral with their staff, though the handsome chauffeur waited outside the church, being a heathen (Edward often claimed to his fellow staff that the church patted itself heartily on the back with one hand while skillfully picking the pockets of parishioners with the other). Clotilda Schulze, the chamber maid, being German, attended a Lutheran church a short streetcar ride from the house.

The day's service was truly ostentatious: George Cardinal Mundelein's pontifical mass of welcome to the congregants. Mundelein had been Archbishop of Chicago since 1915 and Pope Pius XI had only recently made him the cardinal at Santa Maria del Popolo, an Augustinian church in Rome. The cardinal wore scarlet vestments and the flickering light from rows of tapers lit up his joyful countenance. Rows of nuns, staring out glassy-eyed from their wimples, and fresh-faced young monks crammed the rows of the nave of Holy Name, in addition to the usual elderly and wizened men from local monasteries.

Among the nuns were the Dominican Sisters; Sisters of Mercy; Sisters of Providence; Sisters of Notre Dame; of Mary of Nazareth; of the Holy Child; of St. Nancy's Orphanage for Wayward Boys; and of the Resurrection. Mundelein addressed the nuns first, with a message from the Holy Father: "Our religious women are a constant source of consolation to me; without them our progress would be halted and hampered." Mundelein, having tossed this pontifical bone to the nuns, who smiled and shuffled in their pews, suspected that the Pope's gratitude moistened the chasm between the legs. He especially enjoyed titillating the older nuns.

Charlotte's thoughts drifted from the heavily scented pontifications to her roof garden; she fretted over her tomatoes showing signs of mosaic disease. Soon after the church had refused to say the Requiem Mass for her parents because of the nature of their passing, Charlotte had stopped listening to priests, though she attended mass every Sunday, for her sisters' sake rather than her own.

Maude daydreamed her paintings were exhibited at Chicago's Art Institute. She disliked religious art, which seemed oppressive with its speared sides, heads on platters, not to mention colicky infant messiahs.

Amelia also ignored the Latin; she was adrift in a coracle floating in an azure sea off the coast of Mykonos with a basket of Eckert's cakes.

IF THE CLAM sisters truly conversed, which they patently didn't, they would all have realized the emptiness Christian faith offered each of them and they might have spent Sunday mornings doing something far more engaging. As it was, each of them felt beholden to the other two. When the lengthy mass was over, the congregants poured through the heavy bronze doors of Holy Name Cathedral and trickled down side streets toward home or the taverns.

As they strolled back to the house, Mr. Dobson, the proprietor of Kaempfer's bird store on Randolph Street, approached the sisters and doffed his hat.

"Good morning, ladies. Miss Charlotte, you may be interested to know that I'm expecting a special delivery tomorrow of something that may captivate you. A blue spong."

"A spong?" Charlotte asked.

Amelia sniffed. "What's a spong?"

Maude thought she knew. "It's some sort of parrot?"

"No, no. Dear me. It's hard to explain. Far better for you to see it yourself. Come around Tuesday morning? I promise not to show it to another soul until then."

The sisters debated the merits of blue-feathered birds for the rest of their walk.

ON TUESDAY MORNING Edward drove Charlotte to Kaempfer's store on Randolph Street, nestled between O'Connor & Goldberg's, which sold imported French heels, and Henry C. Lytton & Sons, where Mr. Clam once spent a small fortune purchasing matching English dinner suits for him and his chauffeur. Charlotte stepped down from the green Buick convertible, steadied herself on the sidewalk, and brushed from her countenance the dust of the streets. A Mexican double-yellow-headed parrot eyed her from the store's window under an advertisement for Birdolene, "a tonic for your canary—your bird cannot peep without pep." Above the window, yellow letters stretched across a black awning read: "Four years before Lincoln was inaugurated president, Kaempfer's bird store was established in 1857." Charlotte pushed the door open, to be greeted by a chorus of birds squawking and cages rattling.

Dobson walked from the back room, "Ah, Miss Charlotte, you've come to see the blue spong."

"I must admit, Mr. Dobson, I have come to solve the mystery."

"And a mystery it is, my dear. Please wait here." Dobson scuttled off into a back room and soon returned with a ten-inch round brass birdcage, complete with a perch and swing. But instead of a bird resting on the wooden perch, a sphere, a blue ball, balanced there.

Charlotte peered through the bars of the cage. "Oh!" She did not hide her disappointment. The sphere wasn't even a remarkable shade of blue. Not a jay or a thrush or Nicobar pigeon.

"Ah, before you judge, you should witness its trick."

"Does it speak?" Mother once owned a cockatoo that spoke such odd German words. Charlotte had asked Clotilda what "Klemme mein Gesäß" meant but the woman remained tight-lipped.

"Not a word."

The spong then pulsated—*throbbed* might be more apt—until its unique shade of blue light rebounded off the walls of Kaempfer's bird store—*zip zip zip*. Before the rays ran out of steam and faded, Charlotte had jumped back, clutched her three-string pearl necklace, and emitted a volley of stifled screams. "My goodness! I've never seen anything like that before. What is it, Mr. Dobson?"

"It's a blue spong."

"Yes, you have repeatedly made that claim. But *what is it*? It's clearly not a bird."

Mr. Dobson chewed on his mustache. "I'm afraid I don't know what it is. The packing slip that accompanied the crate was in Chinese, a language I'm unfamiliar with."

Hygiene, Charlotte thought. She often thought that birds must have a poor sense of smell not to be bothered by Mr. Dobson's personal essence.

"What does it eat?"

"Nothing."

"Nothing?"

"Not a thing." Dobson smiled.

"And it's from China?"

"I bought it from a man called Wong Sing Fook. He assured me that this is the only blue spong in America. Perhaps," Mr. Dobson said in a low voice, stepping nearer, so that Charlotte could hear him whisper, smell his bad breath, "I think it's likely this is the only blue spong anywhere in the world."

Charlotte brought a gloved hand up to her nose, as if to stifle a sneeze. "And how much do you want for such a curious creature?" If it didn't eat, didn't sing, it seemed harmless enough. Except for those sudden throbbings.

"Eleven dollars and fifty cents. The cage is extra, of course."

Charlotte opened her purse, handed Dobson an agreeable sum, and waited for him to pen a receipt. "And please write down the address of Mr. Wong Sing Fook? I'd like to find out more about the blue spong."

Mr. Dobson grinned. "I'll send the boy around with the spong this afternoon."

AMELIA SAT IN the drawing room with Caitlin, the Clams' housekeeper, going over the week's appointments. Caitlin held Palourde Parlor together, oiled its wheels, repaired its broken cogs, tinkered with its hydraulics, then buffed up its spindles and sprockets with a chamois cloth. Without this plump little Irish woman the Clam sisters would have faltered long ago. They were helpless without her.

"…and Thursday, you are attending the Chicago Women's Club meeting where Miss Alma Binzel will speak on the subject of 'Educational Ideals in the Training of the Very Young Child.'"

Caitlin rustled a stack of papers. "Then on Friday it's another lunch with the Chicago Federation of Women's Organizations at the Sherman Hotel, where the new president Mrs. Edward S. Bailey will speak—"

"At great length, I wouldn't be surprised. Oh, Caitlin, this all sounds so dreadfully boring."

"But, miss, your mother belonged to the club."

"But I'm not my mother. What are Charlotte and Maude doing this week?"

"Charlotte is attending a lecture on the history, use and care of silver in the home at the Hamilton Park Women's Club and Maude is—"

"Oh stop, stop! Just hearing this fatigues me."

The housekeeper jumped at the chill of rebellion that settled in the drawing room.

"Who's that knocking on the door?"

Caitlin headed for the hallway, but Celie, the athletic Polish parlor maid with arms like legs of mutton, reached the door first.

A skinny boy stood on the doorstep. "I have a package for Miss Charlotte Clam. It's from Mr. Dobson at Kaempfer's Bird Store."

Celie thought the boy looked disheveled. As if he'd been through a fight. Or a passionate romp, and barely composed himself before rapping on the door. In truth, it was the latter, as the boy had peeked under the cloth that covered the blue spong. Its light marveled him, entranced him, and he found himself more tumescent than ever before—more so than when he'd admired the face of Rudolph Valentino. He could not very well show up on a Kaempfer customer's doorstep in such a state of arousal, so he had found a convenient alleyway in which to relieve the tension. The man who soon accosted him had originally wanted to rob the busy youth, but the spong throbbed in time with the delivery boy's dorsal veins. Soon the would-be hugger-mugger was on his knees. The spong enjoyed observing virginity lost.

"Run upstairs and find Miss Charlotte." Caitlin motioned to Celie, "And then take this boy downstairs for a sandwich. He's wasting away."

"Miss Charlotte is here." Charlotte skipped down the stairs. She pressed a coin into the boy's sweaty palm and took the covered birdcage. The boy handed her a stained piece of paper on which was written: *Wong Sing Fook, 333 W. 22nd Street.*

Amelia popped her head around the drawing room door. "Another bird?"

Charlotte smiled. "Not quite. All will be revealed this afternoon. Caitlin, can you arrange for tea on the rooftop at four o'clock?

Amelia, you must come, and Maude too." Charlotte glanced around. "Oh, where the deuce is Maude?"

"She's in her studio." Caitlin patted her hair with her fat fingers. They were like sausages. "I'll tell her about tea."

WHAT WAS ONCE a ballroom on the third floor now served as Maude's studio, a cluttered mess of canvases, drop cloths, rags, brushes soaking in oil, and splattered paints. Maude stood back and examined the painting of the Drake Hotel propped up on an easel. It occurred to her how ugly the building was. She hadn't noticed before. A modern structure in the Italian Renaissance style, it resembled a penitentiary with rows of regimented windows. The hotel guests could be criminals, thugs, thieves, murderers and rapists. Why was she painting it? She stepped back. "Focus, focus," she muttered to herself as she pressed her brow. Her mood had yet to recover from Charlotte's unkind remarks about Minnie Fish-Griffin's piano recital.

Minnie was Maude's dearest friend. After Saturday night's recital, while guests descended on the buffet, Maude searched for Minnie, who had slipped away. She found her alone in a side room, where she heaped effusive praise on her friend's piano playing.

"You were just splendid, Minnie, I'm so happy for you. The evening was a great success."

And then Minnie surprised her by leaning forward and kissing Maude. Not on the cheek but square on the lips, a kiss that lasted a second or two longer than could ever be respectable. This kiss unsettled Maude. And the expression Minnie wore immediately afterward seemed like a promise rather than a jest.

Maude had recovered quickly, mentioning how very late she was, and departed before that promise could be fulfilled.

She tried to put the gesture out of her mind, but the kiss haunted her like a phantasm, calling her from the other side of a door she dared not open.

Three rapid knocks on the door broke Maude's maudlin reverie.

Caitlin was on the other side. "I'm sorry to bother you, Miss Maude, but Miss Charlotte has asked me to tell you that tea will be served at four o'clock on the roof. She has something to show you."

"Oh does she? Is this something that I might actually want to see? I wager it's some silly parrot."

Maude's angry tones shocked Caitlin. There had never before been even a hint of animosity between the Clam sisters. Everyone agreed they were far too mediocre for such feelings.

WHEN CHARLOTTE HAD news to announce she would summon her sisters to the rooftop for afternoon tea. At the last "lofty tea," two weeks earlier, Charlotte announced her *Salvia splendens* had bloomed two months earlier than she anticipated. "Of course, it dies with the first frost of winter, but flowering this early means we can enjoy it all the longer." And the tea before that had been when Charlotte received an invitation to the wedding of an old school friend. The nuptials were in Indianapolis. Should she go? After much discussion she decided it was too far. Traveling was fraught with problems. Bandits could board the train, or worse, bears. In wintertime the sisters wore furs, a shivering Edward would shield the sandwiches from wind and snow with a massive umbrella, and the tea had frozen in the china cups before being sipped on more than one occasion.

THAT AFTERNOON WAS hot and humid. The Clam sisters sat in a shady corner amidst the twisting vines, pots of herbs, and cages of linnets, canaries, and parrots. Maude fanned herself with a three-stick fuchsia-colored ostrich-feather fan her late mother had bought for the opera. A bothersome fly was hastily dispatched to the afterlife by a thwack from Amelia's black slipper-satin purse. Spread out before them, three glasses and a jug of lemonade, a platter of cheese and meat sandwiches, spice muffins and Scotch shortbread, all prepared by Bianka and carried upstairs by Celie and Clotilda.

Amelia stirred her glass. "Now, Charlotte, show us this new bird. You're being very secretive about it. Is it another nightingale?"

"It's not a bird at all. Prepare yourself for a surprise." Charlotte lifted the cloth over the birdcage to reveal the blue spong.

"Oh my goodness." Maude pressed her face to the cage. "What an odd little thing."

Now Amelia was interested. "What is it?"

The spong throbbed and glowed. The Clam sisters circled the cage like Macbeth's witches around their bubbling cauldron of intrigue. The spong throb, throb, a-throbbed, then exploded, sending blue light into the afternoon sunshine above Palourde Parlor. Maude screamed once, then passed out cold. Her mother's opera fan flew over the parapet into the garden below (Celie, taking out the garbage, caught the fan before it hit the ground). Amelia yelped, laughed nervously as she covered her eyes. And at that moment, Charlotte decided to visit Chinatown.

THREE

Much later, months really, each of the sisters briefly wondered if Palourde Parlor took an immediate dislike to its newest occupant. They struggled to recall if the house groaned more, the floorboards creaked louder, the doors slammed. Actually, Palourde Parlor loathed the cosmic acupuncture needle of blue light. But, as a house, it could do little to keep something out once it already was in. And the spong began to release exceptionalism into the Clams' dreary existence as if it were grit for the oyster to lacquer.

Charlotte canceled her Thursday appointment to attend the Hamilton Park Women's Club lecture on the history, use and care of silverware. Caitlin was visibly upset. The Clam sisters never canceled appointments. The Clam sisters existed to keep appointments. Caitlin pleaded that Charlotte's mother had been one of the club's most prominent members. There might be repercussions. The Clams' commitment to polishing silver might be called into question.

"You know what those women are like," Caitlin huffed and folded her arms across her chest.

But Charlotte was adamant. She had a pressing engagement elsewhere. She even enjoyed saying it. "I have a pressing engagement elsewhere." A breath of freedom kissed her cheek; she had felt it that afternoon on the roof during tea.

"May I ask where you are going?"

"No, you may not."

"Can I tell Bianka you will be home for dinner?

"Most likely that will be the case. Oh, stop fussing, Caitlin."

The sweet smell of chaos hung in the stairwell of the hallway at Palourde Parlor. Caitlin noticed it. The odor reeked of roses at the moment of decay.

She swooned. She held on tightly to the banister as her nipples tingled. She reddened. Her thoughts turned to bananas. She reddened more.

CHARLOTTE BOARDED A streetcar to the South Side of Chicago, to Chinatown at 22nd St. and Archer. It was her first streetcar ride. The first for any Clam sister. She held on tightly to the rail with one hand and to her hat with the other. She had told no one of her expedition. The blue spong was *her* mystery and she clutched the enigma lovingly to her breast like a Raggedy Ann doll.

The streetcar was empty except for an elderly woman rifling through her purse for a powder puff and a man sporting Oxford bags, a single-breasted jacket, a fedora and a pair of brown and white wingtips, who whistled "Carrickfergus" with all the heart-tugging emotion the song deserved.

Charlotte had never visited Chinatown before, though she had read the Fu-Manchu serial in the *Chicago Tribune*, as well as news items about the tong wars between the Hip Sing and the On Leong. The streetcar rattled to a halt and Charlotte stepped onto 22nd Street, a bustling thoroughfare. She pushed her way past the chop-suey joints, joss houses, teashops and curio emporiums. Peering through the grimy apothecary windows, she marveled at trays of dried lizards, most efficacious for treating dyspepsia, dried centipedes for blistering, and other herbs and roots. Trays in the grocery stores overflowed with dried fish, oysters, mushrooms, clams and chicken gizzards, all adding to the potency of strange smells in Chinatown. Hard-boiled eggs coated in mud and clay. Reputedly, their flavor was as strong as Limburger cheese. She also counted eight types of potatoes preserved in earthen jars.

Charlotte continued along 22nd Street until she came to *333* scrawled on a black door, next to a strip of wood painted in red and gold Chinese characters. Inside, an elderly woman fussed over a pillowcase. Charlotte pushed open the door, setting off a peal of tinkling bells.

"Excuse me, I'm looking for a Mr. Wong Sing Fook. Am I correct in thinking this is where I can find him?" Charlotte was nervous.

With the gaze of a dead fish, the old woman stared at her until Charlotte worried it might be best if she abandoned her quest. But as the last of her resolve began to erode, the old woman smiled as if she had only just recognized a long-lost friend. . "Come this way, Máochóng, you are expected."

Charlotte was led to a heavy door etched with a fearsome dragon, flames shooting from the creature's mouth, threatening to set the doorjamb alight. She passed through, and was met by a handsome Chinaman wearing a black silk shirt, pants and slippers. He looked to be in his thirties. Charlotte felt light-headed from the incense burning in jars. Jasmine, yes, and something more intoxicating.

"Are you Mr. Wong Sing Fook?"

He smiled but shook his head. "No, I am Chin Ming. I am here to welcome you into this house. Please, Miss Clam, step this way. I will take you to meet Wong Sing Fook." His pronunciation was excellent for a foreigner.

They walked a narrow corridor punctuated at regular intervals on both sides by bamboo curtains offering brief glimpses of dimly lit cubicles. The tunnel led to a large gallery lit by row upon row of candles stacked on shelves. By the flickering light, Charlotte noticed heavy tapestries on the walls, rugs beneath her feet, panels decorated with exotic birds and flowers, and a row of six empty cots. "Please lie here…you can rest. I will find Mr. Wong."

Charlotte lowered herself onto a cot, stretched out her legs, leaned back and rested her head on a bolster. Her insides trembled with giddiness. The quivering heat from the countless candles swept her cheeks and neck. She drifted into sleep. When she awoke a young man lay on the cot next to her.

"My name is Wong Sing Fook and you are Charlotte." His teeth were blackened. "You've come to ask me questions about the blue spong. We were expecting you."

"How did you know I would come?"

The question hung in the air unanswered.

"We should smoke."

An old man walked over and knelt between the two cots. With a steady hand he lit a brass lamp. After screwing brass bowls into two sixteen-inch bamboo pipes, he dropped a bead of opium the size of a pea into each of the bowls, then handed one each to Charlotte and Fook. The Chinaman put the pipe to his lips and inhaled the smoke.

Charlotte had, of course, read lurid tales of opium dens in the newspapers and penny dreadfuls. She had also found a copy of Thomas De Quincey's *Confessions of an English Opium Eater* on a high shelf in her father's library. As she took the pipe from Fook, she remembered a line from De Quincey: "Whereas wine disorders the mental faculties, opium introduces amongst them the most exquisite order, legislation and harmony. Wine robs a man of self-possession; opium greatly invigorates it." The moment of her first breath, caution and inhibition dissolved like sugar in boiling water.

A thread of purple vapor spiraled up from the pipe's bowl and Charlotte fell back into Fook's arms. Her eyelids now heavy with the drug, she slipped through time and space until she stood in an orchard with Fook by her side, holding her hand. Plum trees grew as far as the eye could see, heavy with blossom, a thick carpet of pink petals lay beneath Charlotte's feet. Nearby, a squadron of dragonflies protected an ornamental pond of koi and lotus flowers. The clickety-click drone of the dragonflies' brittle wings provided an aural wall to keep evil spirits at bay.

Wong Sing Fook let go of Charlotte's hand, then turned and walked into a mirror. Charlotte reached out for him a moment too late. Startled by the sight, Charlotte turned away and noted a rotund man in flowing robes walking through the trees toward her. On one hand he wore a leather glove fitted tightly up to the elbow. The man stopped and scanned the skies. He whistled to a falcon hovering above the plum trees. The bird flew down and perched on his arm. Kublai Khan, the emperor of China, smiled, then, gently stroking the falcon's chest, he beckoned Charlotte closer. She stepped forward and tried to speak, but the words melted in her throat. They tasted like pomegranates. The emperor opened a small door in the bird's chest to reveal a spong nestling inside. Charlotte's question was answered. The spong she had purchased from Mr. Dobson at Kaempfer's bird store and now lived at Palourde Parlor could only be the beating heart of one of Kublai Khan's prized hawks.

Charlotte did not hesitate to suckle on the pipe again.

It was five minutes till the witching hour when Charlotte returned to Palourde Parlor, disheveled from her opium travels in Chinatown. Caitlin and Edward waited in the hallway. Amelia and Maude had retired to bed an hour earlier, to be woken at midnight if their sister had not returned. Charlotte's disappearance had caused consternation, as the Clam sisters never ventured out at night without a chaperone. This was new. The old rules snapped like dry twigs on the forest floor.

"Oh, Miss Charlotte!" Caitlin wrung her hands. "We were worried about you. We thought perhaps you had been kidnapped into the white slave trade..."

"Oh, don't be ridiculous. Stop fussing!" Charlotte breezed through the hallway and skipped up the stairs. "I'm quite old enough to look after myself. Go to bed."

THE FOLLOWING DAY Charlotte woke early, watered the plants, and tended to her birds. Jessie, her lorikeet, was particularly vocal and perky: "Jessie's a good girl, Jessie's a good girl." It was still dark outside, though the sun was rising over Lake Michigan, giving an orange aura to the buildings along the shoreline. Wearing red silk pajamas, Charlotte danced barefoot in her rooftop garden, welcoming the goddess Aurora. She attempted a *pas de basque* near the "Dorothy Perkins" arbor and a *pas de ciseaux* near the cane rocker, followed by *demi-plié*, *temps de cuisse*, *fermé* and ending with Mikhail Fokine's *The Dying Swan* to Camille Saint-Saëns's cello solo *Le Cygne* from *Le Carnaval des Animaux*. Charlotte reached into the cage and cradled the blue spong in the palm of her hand. She held the spong close to her chest, two heartbeats merging as one. She then threw the spong into the air, where it hovered briefly over an armchair, shot like a meteor across the room, pulsated half a dozen times, then exploded with light.

Charlotte whispered under her breath, "The beating heart of a hawk should fly free, and not be trapped in a cage."

Charlotte bathed and dressed, then descended the stairs with the blue spong hovering above her right shoulder like a punctuation mark. Amelia and Maude were already seated at the breakfast table when Charlotte entered.

"Oh, good morning, Charlotte, and good morning, spong." Amelia eyed the spong.

"How does one correctly address a spong?" Maude asked. "I don't want to offend."

"I think good morning, spong, should be enough. I've decided to let the spong fly around the house free, as a guest."

"Aren't you worried it might fly away?" Amelia picked up a slice of toast. It dangled from her fingertips.

"I think the spong should be free to make its own decisions. If it wants to fly away, it will, and if it wants to stay, then it will stay."

Amelia and Maude did not mention Charlotte's late arrival the previous night. They assumed all would be revealed at the proper time. There would be a perfectly good explanation as to why Charlotte had arrived home at midnight. The spong lingered near a painting by the watercolorist Gifford Beal of a man fishing in a river.

"I think the spong is looking at me." Amelia was unsettled.

Maude reassured her. "Don't be anile. How could something without eyes look at you?"

"No, it's definitely looking at me. Charlotte, I hear from Caitlin that you canceled the Hamilton Park Women's Club lecture on the history, use and care of silver yesterday. How brave of you." Amelia buttered the slice of toast and took a bite.

"Yes, it was rather brave of me, wasn't it?"

"Well, I've been rather brave too." Maude straightened herself in the chair. "I've canceled a charity event this afternoon. I was supposed to be fundraising for the Art Institute to buy the Gilbert Stuart portrait of George Washington. However, they will have to raise the money without me. I have another appointment. I'm meeting Minnie Fish-Griffin for tea this afternoon. We're going to the Green Mask."

Charlotte was taken aback. "Isn't that where the theatrical crowd go? Where the men are somewhat temperamental."

"Yes."

"And the women smoke cigars?" Amelia was equally as shocked as Charlotte.

"I may start smoking cigars myself." Maude pretended to light a cigar. She coughed loudly. The three Clam sisters laughed. "And then after tea, Minnie and I are going to see a vaudeville show at the Randolph Theater. Here, it's advertised in the paper. *Daughters of Today*, it's called."

"That sounds rather..." Amelia trailed off, lost for words.

"I, too, have plans this evening." Charlotte twisted a ring on her finger. "I'm going to a Chinese opera with my gentleman friend, Chin Ming. The opera is called *The Peach Blossom Fan* and it's in Chinatown. Another friend, Wong Sing Fook, is performing in it. You remember I told you I was going to find out more about our blue spong, well, Mr. Dobson at Kaempfer's bird store told me he obtained it from a Mr. Wong Sing Fook in Chinatown. And so yesterday I visited him and we've become firm friends."

A forkful of scrambled eggs froze on its journey from the plate to Amelia's mouth. Maude turned pale. She asked, "You went to Chinatown? By yourself?"

Charlotte nodded.

Amelia set down her fork. "But they're...they're...so thin-eyed." She tsked. "I dislike how they look at us."

"I'll have you know that Wong Sing Fook is perfectly respectable. He's an actor."

The younger Clam sisters' eyes opened.

"He's currently appearing in *The Peach Blossom Fan*. I believe the role is Li Xiangjun, a courtesan, and the story is about her love for a young scholar named Hou Fangyu. The opera takes place during the decline of the Ming Dynasty."

"*He* plays a courtesan?" asked Amelia.

"It's like a prostitute," Maude said.

"I know what a courtesan is." Amelia struggled to maintain her composure. "So he is a female impersonator?"

Charlotte dabbed at the corners of her mouth with a napkin. "Yes. I once heard Father telling Edward that Chicago often entertained such…entertainers before the turn of the century. On their way out west."

Maude was in shock. "And what about the other man?"

"Chin Ming?"

"Yes."

Charlotte offered a slip of a smile. "Chin Ming is the leader of the Hip Sing."

Before her sisters could ask, she said, "Rather like a fraternal order. Only, they are a Chinese crime gang. He's also the proprietor of several opium dens. Prominent ones."

The blue spong throbbed and throbbed, then exploded, sending out shards of steel-blue light that ricocheted off the walls of the dining room at Palourde Parlor.

Maude and Amelia reached for each other's hands, gasped for air, as they struggled to accept what they'd just heard their sister say.

FOUR

Charlotte kept her opium dream a secret. After all, the blue spong was *her* mystery. There was another secret too. Chin Wing had seduced her, taken her innocence, caused her to shudder with ecstatic spasms on the floor cushions in his apartment. Then, after tea and Huangqiao sesame-seed cake, his bodyguards drove Charlotte home to Palourde Parlor and escorted her to the door.

Maude savored the memory of Minnie Fish-Griffin's kiss as the two strolled arm in arm into the Green Mask. The café was busy with an eclectic crowd, artists and writers, a smattering of vaudeville and circus acts, and a group of rowdy male students from Northwestern University. They were guided to an empty table. An effete young man with scarlet lips, a white-powdered girlish face, wearing a French voile blouse and baggy Syrian pants, brought them a tray with a teapot, cups, and sandwiches. "There are two kinds of sandwiches. These over here contain thin slices of cucumber, a layer of mayonnaise and finely chopped dates, and these are sardine paste mixed with butter and lemon juice. My name is Philip, or Phyllis, whichever you prefer, and I am your waitress for the duration of your visit to the Green Mask. I insist you immerse yourself in the complete and utter madness of it all."

A crapulent woman at the next table squealed with laughter. Phyllis pirouetted twice, then floated into the kitchen like a feather on a breeze, leaving a dusting of face powder hanging in the air.

Maude felt her tongue wince. "This tea is very odd tasting."

Minnie giggled. "That's because it contains juniper fruit."

Maude gasped. "You don't mean…"

Minnie mouthed *G-I-N.*

"But what about the Volstead Act?"

"It doesn't exist here. There are many unacceptable things that are quite acceptable at the Green Mask. You have to leave your inhibitions at the door. They have no place here."

"It's hard to believe the Green Mask is so close to my house and yet I never knew it was here. Not that I would have entered its portals, if it hadn't been for you, Minnie. I do believe you're leading me astray."

At Palourde Parlor the blue spong twitched as it studied a framed photograph of Maude on a sideboard in the living room. She was sitting on a park bench wearing a voluminous sun hat. She stared vacantly into the camera lens. No smile. No expression. Just a vessel filled to the brim with mediocrity.

Minnie sipped her gin. "I've been coming here for a while. I know the owners, Agnes Weiner and Beryl Boughton, her lady friend. Agnes used to work in a circus, as a snake charmer, and Beryl was an actress in motion pictures at Essanay Film Manufacturing Company here in Chicago. She was in a Charlie Chaplin movie, *Vaudeville on Carmen*, and also with Gloria Swanson in *The Fable of Elvira and Farina and the Meal Ticket.* Then she had an accident on the set, broke both her arms, and the insurance money bought the Green Mask."

A hush fell over the café as a young woman sat before the piano and flexed her fingers. A middle-aged man joined her. He had a five-o'clock shadow and was wearing a little girl's frilly blue dress and a blond wig tied up in pigtails. He introduced himself as Betsy Cuddles, curtseyed to the audience and began to sing:

"In my sweet little Alice blue gown,
When I first wandered down into town,
I was both proud and shy,
As I felt every eye,
But in every shop window I'd primp, passing by."

The students roared with laughter, banging the tables with their fists. "Oh, what a very pretty girlie." A young blond boy no more than eighteen years of age pointed and roared with laughter. "She can come with me to the ice-cream parlor anytime she wants."

"Then in a manner of fashion I'd frown,
And the world seemed to smile all around.
Till it wilted I wore it,

I'll always adore it,
My sweet little Alice blue gown."

The impersonator smiled and curtsied again to deafening applause. Maude and Minnie finished their "tea" and sandwiches, and with high spirits and much laughter they linked arms and skipped along the sidewalk to the Randolph Street Theatre to see *Daughters of Today,* a variety show of slapstick, song-and-dance routines and juggling acts. They were particularly impressed with the comedy double act, Gordon and Delmar. Leaving the theater, Minnie took the part of Gordon and Maude was Delmar.

"My goodness what was that terrible noise?" Minnie feigned surprise.

"That was me, I just fell down a whole flight of stairs."

"You fell down a whole flight of stairs?"

"Oh, that's all right, I was coming down anyway, so it didn't make much difference."

And:

"I sang that song with feeling." Minnie placed her hand on her heart.

"Yes, you must have been feeling pretty bad."

"See here, you have to understand there is music in me."

"Well, there ought to be, I haven't heard any come out."

They laughed together on the sidewalk, arms around each other, bent double.

Minnie hailed a Checker Taxi. "Let's go slumming."

"What's slumming?"

A taxi stopped and the two women climbed in.

"Take us to the Paradise Gardens on 35th Street."

"Isn't that...?"

"Isn't that what?"

"Isn't that where the colored people live?"

The taxi pulled up outside a black-and-tan nightclub in the heart of Bronzeville, a thriving black metropolis on the South Side of Chicago. It was a warm summer night, stars glittering in the sky, and the streets bustling with crowds of sensation-seekers. The two women entered the club under a lighted marquee sign that read: *Mamie Smith and Her Jazz Hounds*, and in smaller lettering underneath, *Joe Winn's Creole Jazz Band*. Inside, they sat in the observation balcony overlooking the dance floor, where men and women, women and women, and men and men, all danced together. After two songs, Joe Winn's Creole Jazz Band left the stage and other musicians walked on. Mamie Smith introduced the band—Coleman "Hawk" Hawkins on saxophone, James “Bubber” Miley on trumpet, the names of the others dissolved into the clouds of cigarette smoke, chatter, and clinking glasses.

Mamie leaned into the microphone. “This song is for any man who thinks they can mess with a girl like me. Not that any of you would be that foolhardy.”

Mamie sang: “He took her home last night … She gave him a kiss … But when he went too far … She upped and told him this … Don’t mess with me, don’t mess with me. Now you work fast, that’s mighty true. You’re in the right church, but in the wrong pew.

“Don’t mess with me, you better run along and let me be. Say listen here, I got a razor, it’s got a nasty blade. You better pass on your Circus. I done seen your parade. I also picked the ground where your body’s gonna be laid.

“Don’t mess with me, you better run along and let me be. If I land on you … oh lord! Next time people talk to you, it’ll be through a Ouija board.

“Don’t mess with me, don’t mess with me.”

Maude was mesmerized. She squeezed Minnie’s hand as the blues woman sang “Just Like You Took My Man Away From Me” and “Remorseful Blues,” then midway through “Jazzbo Ball” all hell broke loose as prohibition cops burst into the club, some with guns drawn, others smashing up the bar, the tables, anything in their path, with axes. Scuffles broke out as revelers were tackled to the ground, arrested and dragged outside. Others were lined up against a wall and searched for hip flasks. One wide-eyed cop grabbed Minnie from behind, but Maude brought a glass ashtray down onto his head. He fell to the floor, blood gushing from a three-inch wound. An hour later the Paradise Gardens was shuttered, customers and staff bundled into patrol wagons heading for the lock-up at Englewood police station.

Minnie held on tightly to Maude. “Say nothing to the police. I can get us out of this.”

looked bedraggled, Miss Amelia."
lraggled?!"
not my place to say, but thoroughly bedraggled. As if she
ı running through the woods, chased by wild animals. Her
vere torn."
ıat moment Caitlin entered the dining room.
tlin, what's this I hear about Maude arriving home
ed?"
s Charlotte arrived home about one o'clock from the
opera, and Miss Maude arrived not so long ago."
king bedraggled."
in hesitated. "Yes, miss. Also her lip was cut and bleeding. I
mpression there had been some kind of brawl."
ıde in a brawl." Amelia leaned back in her chair. She
d if perhaps she had not woken up that morning, and this
conversation was some queer dream. "A brawl. That can't
Maude doesn't brawl. She paints pictures of buildings.
vho paint pictures of buildings don't brawl. The two are
ous."
e say there is a reasonable explanation."
ia looked at Caitlin. "Well, I look forward to hearing it. I
k what's gotten into those two lately."
t had gotten into "those two" was the blue spong.
n took a deep breath. "Miss, if I may: Bianka has been
ing about the blue spong. She says it follows her around the
ıe said it's haunting her. It watches her while she's baking."
ia waved a hand, as if swatting an airborne pest. "It's
talking to me about it. Talk to Charlotte, it's her spong.
you can locate her whereabouts. Try Timbuktu, or up the
River in a canoe. She could be living with headhunters.
never tell these days."
ia unfolded the *Chicago Tribune*. "Look at this, Caitlin,
nightclub raided. Seventy-nine people arrested. It says
e white, seven Chinamen and sixty-three colored.' Six of
ed fellows were masquerading as women. It goes on to
police found two fifty-gallon stills, twenty-five gallons of
en gallons of synthetic gin, twelve cases of beer, five quarts
, four gallons of moonshine, about a pound of opium, four
ines, one dice game.' What is the world coming to?"

ʏ WAS AMELIA'S Eckert's Bakery day, a highlight of her
vas the day she indulged in the decadence of sweetmeats,

FIVE

Two OF THE three Clam sisters had t
away from their mediocre lives. In one e
three new planets orbiting Palourde Parl
artists, poets, actors, "temperamentals" ar
world of slapstick and vaudeville; and
female blues singers who are tough-on
had crawled out of the quicksand of med
to a Chinese gangster. She also chased t
toe into the highbrow world of Chine
vocals and female impersonation. Mea
evening reading *Freckles,* a novel by G
a disabled Chicago orphan hired by tl
Co. to guard lumber in the Limberlos
to succumb to the seduction of the blu
wallow like a hopped-up hippo in a ces

THE FOLLOWING MORNING, Amelia sat
at home, the silence broken only by Ce
tureen of scrambled eggs. A beam of s
net curtains in the Queen Anne-style
platter of muffins.

"Where are Charlotte and Maude t

"They're sleeping late, Miss Amelia

"Late? They never sleep late."

"They both returned home late last
in only half an hour ago and went strai

Amelia stiffened.

"Sh

"Be

"It's
had be
clothes

At

"Ca
bedragg

"Mi
Chines

"Lo

Cai
got the

"Ma
wonder
breakfa
be righ
Ladies
incongr

"I d

Am
can't thi

Wha

Cait
complai
house. S

Ame
pointles
That's if
Orinoco
One can

Ame
another
here, 'ni
the colo
say, 'The
alcohol,
of whisk
slot mac

SATURDA
week. It

pastries and dainties. This was a dark and wicked side of herself she kept from her sisters. Such was Amelia's mediocre existence that eating dessert was sinful. It almost merited an exorcism from a Catholic priest. "Out damn pastry demons! In the name of God leave this poor woman in peace, and take your cakes back with you, back into the bowels of hell."

However, Amelia's mediocrity was soon to crack. On her way to Eckert's Bakery, she cut across Bughouse Square. The soapboxers and hecklers were out in force. As she pushed her way through the rabble she overheard snippets of oratory from impeccably attired religionists of the Moody Bible Institute, be-robed Druids heavy with amulets and spouting mumbo-jumbo, fiery anarchists, advocates of free love, and scruffy, bearded, Industrial Workers of the World lauding Karl Marx. Halfway across the square, Amelia was accosted by a tall skeletal figure, a battered gray derby balanced atop his tousle-headed pate, baggy black pants, and a white shirt with the sleeves rolled up to the elbows.

"What do you know of the starving children of factory workers?" The speaker jabbed an accusing finger at Amelia. "Look at the clothes you wear. You could feed a family for a week on the price of that hat alone."

"Then here is my hat, let them feed on it for a week." Amelia tore off the felt bonnet she'd bought at Chas-A-Stevens & Bros. for five dollars the week before, and threw it at the man.

The crowd roared with laughter. One man shouted. "That hat would be very nice with some gravy and dumplings."

Amelia darted down a side street. She sat on a low wall and breathed deeply. Blood coursed through her veins. She had spoken up. What a dreadful man. He had no right to accost her in the street. She continued to Eckert's Bakery where she bought the usual Angel Divinity Cake, chocolate nougat, and Florida Teas with Lady Baltimore icing. Amelia took a different route home. South on Clark Street, through the heart of Towertown, a bohemian settlement of artists, writers, political radicals, effete young men and masculine women. Outside 817 N. Clark Street she stopped. A crudely painted sign nailed above a red door caught her eye: *The Radical Bookstore*. Amelia peered through the grimy window at a display of books written by authors like Mikhail Bakunin and Peter Kropotkin. Authors unfamiliar to her. She entered into someone's living room, three high-back leather chairs around a small mahogany gate-leg table, the surface hidden beneath a layer of pamphlets and papers. Beyond that, next to a sign reading *Bookshelf Alley*, two rows of rickety bookshelves stretched into the distance. At the far end a woman sat behind a desk.

"I believe in the human intellect," the woman bellowed down Bookshelf Alley. "I believe in demonstrating the value of my own individual type. I believe in demonstrating the value of 'me' to the universe. I am in search of freedom and now, at last, I am free. My name is Lillian Udell and you are very welcome here. Is there anything I can help you with? Howard! Howard! We have a visitor, a revolutionary…or perhaps a skeptic."

A middle-aged bearded man in an ill-fitting crumpled suit peered over his half-moon reading glasses. "Can I help you with anything? My name is Howard Udell. I see you've met my wife who, in case you hadn't noticed, is blind."

"No, I hadn't noticed."

"Blind as a bat, but as shrewd as a fox." Lillian laughed so loud that a slim white leatherbound volume of Lord Byron's poetry trembled.

"I was just passing and I hadn't noticed your bookstore before. I was thinking of browsing, or perhaps you could suggest a book for me to read."

"I can judge your spirit by your voice, and I would say you were of a nervous disposition, and yet there is a sense of adventure in you. I suggest you read *Love and the Gypsy* by Konrad Bercovici. I recommend that not only do you read it and soak up the passion of it, but that you hear him talk about the book at the Gray Cottage tomorrow night."

"The Gray Cottage?"

"Yes, a coffee house at 10 Cass Street, not far from here. It is an oasis of radical thought in a dry desert of indifference."

Amelia bought the book. "Thank you, I will read this, and I will soak up the passion of it, as you suggest, but I cannot hear Bercovici speak at the Gray Cottage. I never go out at night alone. All these gangland shootings, police raids, and beer-runners and bootleggers, it's not safe. Even that nice Mr. O'Banion in the florist store opposite Holy Name Cathedral is now thought to be a scoundrel."

"Then you must come with me." The voice came from behind her. Amelia spun around to be greeted by a young man with a mass of black curly hair, startling hazelnut eyes, and a neatly trimmed mustache.

Amelia took a step back. "Oh! I didn't hear you come in."

"That's because I was already here, sitting in this chair. I was listening to you and I've decided that we must go and see Konrad Bercovici together. It's the only solution. There is no other option. We will protect each other from the gangsters. My name is Antonio

Corigliani and you…your name is?"

"Amelia. Amelia Clam."

"Clam, molluschi…like the shellfish. You must read *Love and the Gypsy* today and tomorrow, and tomorrow evening we must go and hear Bercovici speak together."

"But I don't even know you."

"And you never will, unless you discover the gypsy inside of yourself. There is a gypsy inside all of us, don't you think? A nomadic soul that travels and never stays in one place for long, a spirit that is free and not entangled in one place, one time, or one idea."

"Perhaps." Amelia was intrigued.

"No, I see you are not convinced. Come here. Look here." Antonio gestured toward a mirror on the wall. "Look in this mirror and see the gypsy within you."

Amelia laughed. "I will look into the mirror and if I see a gypsy, I will allow you to escort me to the Gray Cottage, if I don't, then I will not."

"Then look."

What Amelia saw in the mirror was not a gypsy woman, but the blue spong, throb, throb, a-throbbing, and then exploding into steel-blue shards of light.

"Do you see the gypsy?" Antonio held his breath.

"Yes, I do, I see the gypsy very clearly," Amelia lied. It felt grand.

SIX

Charlotte now spent more time in Chinatown with Chin Wing and his family than she did at Palourde Parlor. She was learning Chinese and trying new cuisine, dining on dà tāng huángyú and daa tung hwung-yoo, both easier to eat than pronounce. Meanwhile, Maude was lost in a Sapphic romance with Minnie Fish-Griffin. She visited the Vendome Music Shop at 47 E. 31st Street to begin a collection of Race Records. On Minnie's recommendation, she bought Alberta Hunter's *Bleeding Heart Blues* and Ida Cox's *Chicago Bound Blues.* She had already worn out the stylus on her Victrola. The Sunday-morning breakfast ritual at home was usually a subdued affair. This Sunday, however, the three Clam sisters had ventured beyond the curlicue gates and returned with foreign and exotic ideas. Amelia was first at the table, followed by Maude, who glowed like a firefly on a hot summer night.

"Good morning, Amelia. How are you this fine morning?"

"Very well. I haven't seen you or Charlotte since Friday. Did you enjoy your evening with Minnie Fish-Griffin? Weren't you seeing a play, or was it a show? …Oh, good morning, Charlotte."

Charlotte joined her sisters at the table.

"I was asking Maude about her evening with Minnie. What was the show called?" In truth, Amelia was more interested in why Maude had returned home bedraggled just before dawn.

"It was called *Daughters of Today.* It was a vaudeville show. It was a great deal of fun. Minnie and I particularly liked the comedy routine of Gordon and Delmar and the Nagyfys, who are human salamanders. After the show we went slumming to a club on the South Side and saw Mamie Smith and Her Jazz Hounds."

"Did they bark? The jazz hounds, did they bark?" Charlotte laughed at her own joke.

"They did bark. Yes, in a way. Mamie Smith was wonderful. Then the police raided the club and we were all arrested and taken off to jail. Minnie got us out. Her father owns a chain of department stores and knows the Chief of Police."

Amelia stiffened. "Oh, Maude, I read about that raid in the newspaper yesterday. One of the policemen is in hospital, hit over the head. How could anyone do such a thing?"

Charlotte shuddered. "That must have been awful for you, I can't imagine being locked in a jail cell."

Maude smirked. "It was all quite fun, actually. Minnie and I were locked in a cell with a loose woman, a prostitute. Her name was Nelly Flynn and she told us extraordinary tales about riding crops and men who like to wear horse saddles in the boudoir."

"Really? I wonder if these loose women have to wear spurs?" Amelia reddened at her own words. "I can't believe I just said that."

Maude laughed. "Yes, sometimes they do wear spurs. The establishment she works at is called Miss Sadie's Galloping Stallion Riding Stables for Gentlemen with Equestrian Taste."

A cup shattered on the floor. Celie turned white as a sheet. "I'm sorry, I don't know what I was thinking."

"Oh, don't worry about it, Celie. It's only a cup." Charlotte stared into a bowl of oatmeal and for a moment was lost in thought.

The blue spong hovered over the parlor maid's head and throbbed gently. Celie tried to shoo it away. She was flustered. She hadn't expected to hear mention of Miss Sadie's Galloping Stallion Riding Stables for Gentlemen with Equestrian Taste at the Clams' breakfast table. The subject of men's sporting establishments seemed at odds with stewed prunes, rolled oats, eggs, bacon, bread rolls and Bianka's homemade orange marmalade.

Richard Clam's last will and testament stipulated that the staff at Palourde Parlor be employed on full pay for five years. And with that deadline imminent, Celie had applied for a job advertised in the *Chicago American*, a tabloid of ill repute. The previous day, she'd taken a train to Evanston, then changed at the Church Street terminus, finally catching the Gold Coast Limited to Lake Forest. At the station, Celie was picked up and driven to Miss Sadie's Galloping Stallion Riding Stables for Gentlemen with Equestrian Taste. There she interviewed with Miss Sadie, a woman in her early fifties with jet-black hair pulled back into a tight bun. Though merciless with her clients, Miss Sadie was a kind-hearted soul and maternal toward her "stable of gals."

Celie was asked to wear a derby hat, breeches of light Bedford cord, jodhpurs, black leather boots, and a riding habit. After saddling-up a middle-aged balding banker from Milwaukee, Celie trotted him around the paddock, whipping his bare buttocks with a riding crop. Afterward she rubbed him down in a stable stall.

Nobody knew that beneath the timid exterior, Celestynka "Celie" Majewski was an extreme sadist. Nobody except the blue spong, that is. Since reading the ad in the paper, Celie fought the irresistible urge to punch men in the face. She ran her fingertips over the fleece-lined leather saddle. "Where do you buy these man-saddles?"

"Dreckers Saddlery, they make all our equipment." Miss Sadie was the consummate businesswoman. You would think she was selling used cars rather than running a brothel for men with equestrian tastes.

The balding Milwaukee banker stood up, but Celie cracked the riding crop down on the back of his legs. "Stay down until I tell you otherwise."

Miss Sadie hired Celie on the spot. "You have ruthless eyes, the eyes of a woman with no mercy. Men are wild animals that need to be trained. You will be perfect for breaking in my man-ponies. You will take their spirit and snap it like a twig. You will break them down until they're eating oats out of your hand. It takes a special kind of woman to take a riding crop to a man's testicles. You can start next week."

Celie swept up the pieces of broken crockery.

Charlotte held court at the breakfast table. "Well, while Maude was languishing in prison with prostitutes, I was at the opera."

"A Chinese opera. It sounds wonderful." Amelia clapped her hands.

"Oh it was. It was called *The Peach Blossom Fan*, written in the Qing dynasty by Kong Shangren. Wong Sing Fook played the part of Li Xiangjun exquisitely. You never would have guessed she was a man. It was a beautiful and very sad love story, about how a young couple's love for each other blossomed while everything around them fell into darkness and decay."

Maude pushed a muffin around her plate. "But how did you understand what they were singing?"

"Chin Ming, the friend I was telling you about, accompanied me. He whispered in my ear as the plot unfolded on the stage. Much of it cannot be described in words, so you must go and see the opera yourself. And you, Amelia, how have you been amusing yourself? Didn't you have something with the Chicago Federation of Women's Organizations on Friday?"

"Yes, it was very dull. The new president of the organization, Mrs. Edward S. Bailey, is possibly the dullest woman who ever lived. However, yesterday was much improved, as I had occasion to meet Antonio Corigliani in the Radical Bookstore."

Charlotte looked visibly shaken. "A radical bookstore?"

"It's quite close to here, run by a blind woman. It was there I met Antonio, an Italian anarchist. He's taking me out tonight to hear the writer Konrad Bercovici talk about his new book *Love and the Gypsy*. So today I will be locking myself away and reading the book, which is why I won't be joining you for mass at Holy Name Cathedral." Amelia bit into a slice of toast, then stood up and left the room.

Charlotte and Maude froze, Charlotte holding a fork loaded with scrambled eggs in mid-air and Maude reaching for a jug of orange juice. It was a full minute before either could speak.

"An anarchist." Charlotte's scrambled eggs fell off the fork. "Father would be horrified."

"But Father isn't here, is he?" Maude picked up the jug of orange juice and poured herself a glass. She wondered if Father was in Hell. "I think it's all terribly exciting. Amelia will be learning how to make bombs soon. And she'll be consorting with Miss Emma Goldman and her riotous rabble of revolutionaries."

Charlotte turned white.

"What's wrong?"

"I forgot to warn Amelia, there's a tattooed Chinaman in the servants' quarters."

The *Chicago Tribune* headline read: "Tong Wars in Chinatown escalate." Charlotte, a Hip Sing leader's lover, was now a target. Lin Kwang, her bodyguard, now resided in the servants' quarters at Palourde Parlor with a Thompson submachine gun. Kwang followed Charlotte like a well-armed puppy dog. A few days earlier, Charlotte tended vines in her rooftop garden and hosted afternoon teas. Now she was on an On Leong hit list. When the blue spong dissolved mediocrity, it did so with a ruthless efficiency, like pouring acid onto a primrose.

SEVEN

Love happened at first sight for each Clam sister: Charlotte with Chin Wing, leader of a Chinese gang; Maude with Minnie Fish-Griffin, a rebel without a cause; and Amelia with Antonio Corigliani, an Italian anarchist. The Clams' lovers were free spirits, unaffected by the debilitating disease of mediocrity. Each of them enticed a sister away from the mundane by the promise of delicious madness and chaos.

The blue spong hovered about Bianka, a woman who embraced not just the everyday but even the contours of normality. Mediocrity was a treasured doll she held tightly to her chest. A rigid culinary routine, uninterrupted by aspirations, ambitions and dreams, was all she had. She feared change as if it were a boogeyman ready to pounce and devour her if she strayed into the shadows.

The spong hovered over the sink. Bianka shooed it away with her favorite spatula, one that had served her well with various sauces. Tiny marks marred the very tip. Marks left by her incisors.

She lured the spong into a closet and then slammed the door shut. That was when she discovered the blue spong passed through walls like the ghost of murdered children, unable to cross over to the other side, and haunting houses. All the new activity at Palourde Parlor unsettled her, disrupted her routine. Usually, every day was the same, set in stone. Caitlin gave the Clams a dinner menu at the breakfast table and they approved or altered it. That was the way of things, but the recent comings and goings destroyed all that. Bianka now prepared dinner for six every night, three Clam sisters and three guests, whether there was anyone there to eat it or not. When not, the staff at Palourde Parlor dined on the finest beefsteak and kidney pie with vegetables, followed by desserts like lemon sorbet and mixed fruits dipped in bowls of melted chocolate.

After breakfast, Caitlin walked alone to Holy Name Cathedral. There, she entered the confessional and told the priest she had performed an indecent act on a heathen. The priest's jaw dropped like it had been dislocated in a bar brawl. He was speechless for a full minute. Then he asked for more specifics. Yes, the act had been one of carnal behavior. Yes, it had been done willingly. Yes, neither she nor the heathen—whose ethnicity she now described—were married. Yes, the Chinaman had a significant foreskin. Yes, she had thought of God while her head bobbed and she was on her knees.

Words of admonishment lodged in his throat like a fishbone. He had taken Caitlin's confession for years but never heard anything like this before. She once owned up to stealing a cookie. Another time, she wished someone ill will. The plump Irish woman with the sausage fingers was a model of propriety. Respectable. Highbrow. Not someone who orally pleased the Yellow Menace.

The blue spong lurked in the nave of the church, throb throb a-throbbing, sending out light.

The previous night, Charlotte had introduced Caitlin to Lin Kwang, her bodyguard. "Lin Kwang will be staying with us for the foreseeable future. Please give him one of the bedrooms in the servants' quarters."

Caitlin took Lin Kwang to a bedroom, where the blue spong hid behind the lace drapes throb throb a-throbbing.

"You will have to ignore the blue spong, it's Miss Charlotte's pet. She lets it fly free around the house."

Lin Kwang smiled. "Oh, I know about the blue spong. There are many Chinese legends about it. Many stories. Let me show you." Lin Kwang removed his shirt, showing Caitlin a tattoo of the blue spong on his back. "You see, it's flying over the mountains in search of adventure."

"Oh, yes, and there's a woman here, standing by this tree. She looks sad. Why is she sad?"

"Because her life is one of mediocrity. She has no ambition, no fire in her soul. The fire has been doused. And look here." Lin Kwang turned and on his chest were three warriors on horseback, one rearing up, aiming a crossbow. "This tattoo tells the story of the Wu Hu uprising. And here..." Lin Kwang turned again and dropped his pants to show two fearsome tigers on his buttocks. Then he turned back to show Caitlin a red fire-breathing dragon on his erect member. "Have you ever kissed a dragon?"

"No, never."

"They say if you kiss a dragon much wealth will come to you." Lin Kwang's member throbbed and throbbed and throbbed, until the spong exploded with light ricocheting off the walls of the tiny bedroom, fizzling out like snakes on fire.

Caitlin knelt and kissed the dragon. Then she swallowed the fearsome reptile with its scaly skin, giant wings and fiery breath. She had a ten dollar bill to prove it. She slipped the bill into her purse. It went into her "Rainy Day Fund."

Bianka excused herself from Sunday mass. She visited David Podmore, a noted medium with the International Spiritualist Church. Bianka had read an article by Podmore in the *Chicago Tribune* in which he argued Jesus Christ was clairvoyant, his twelve apostles psychics. He argued Simon the Zealot found water in the desert with a divining rod and Bartholomew juggled clay pots with his mind. Podmore also claimed he talked to the dead. For years, Bianka had a recurring dream her deceased parents were trying to contact her from beyond the grave. In their case it was a watery grave, as they drowned in the German U-Boat attack on the RMS *Lusitania* on May 7, 1915. A fifteen-year-old Bianka survived the icy waters, returning to America to live with a maiden aunt in New York, who died two weeks later. Another aunt in Chicago, who owned several trattorias, took her in and taught her to cook. Sadly, a disagreement over a recipe for *pasta con le sarde* reached boiling point, leading Bianka to take employment with the Clams.

Bianka turned onto Argyle Street. She was deafened by the metallic buzz of cicadas in the trees. It was an industrial factory noise. The screech of metal on metal reminded her of living in New York with her aunt near the Oneida Machine Twist and Sewing Silk Co. She cringed at the memory. On Podmore's doorstep, she lifted the brass wolf's-head knocker, bringing it down three times. A tall thin woman opened the door, a shock of red hair tumbling to her waist. She wore emerald-green robes, brown sandals and heavy jewelry: a silver, crystal, and black suede cuff, a mottled blue glass necklace and matching ring, and encircling her pate a silver tiara headpiece. She bore a striking resemblance to Dante Gabriel Rossetti's *Beata Beatrix*, the painting depicting Beatrice Portinari at the moment of her death, from Dante Alighieri's poem "La Vita Nuova."

Bianka heard her mother's voice in the breeze:

"E sì come la mente mi ridice, Amor mi disse: 'Quell'è Primavera, E quell'ha nome Amor, sì mi somiglia.'"

Words from "La Vita Nuova." What did it all mean? Bianka brushed it aside and steadied herself against the doorjamb. She felt faint, overwhelmed by a wave of dark sinister magic. She closed her eyes, but all she could see was the blue spong throb, throb, a-throbbing. Visiting a clairvoyant grated against her Catholicism. It was meddling in the supernatural. In the Middle Ages she would be tried by the Witchfinder General, found guilty, then burned at the stake. Bianka bristled with the spirit of Joan of Arc, La Pucelle d'Orléans.

"Please come in. My name is Persephone, named after the Greek Goddess of the Underworld...a curse and a blessing, you might say. I am David Podmore's assistant and you must be Bianka Morietta. "

Persephone led Bianka into a Victorian sitting room, cluttered with potted plants, dusty furniture, wallpaper with garish red poppies, and a sideboard crammed with photographs of grim-faced family members. Heavy drapes drawn against the morning sunlight. A man in his early fifties sat upright at a table, his face lit by a dozen flickering candles. The air was thick with sandalwood incense. The man's hands, long feminine fingers, lay folded neatly like tree roots on the tabletop. He attempted a smile, the tight line of his gray lips arched upwards at the corners, but not enough to convey joy. It was the smile of a corpse in the throes of rigor mortis.

"Please sit down, Miss Morietta. My name is David Podmore and I understand you wish to make contact with your parents on the far side of death's curtains. I understand they died on the *Lusitania*. That was a terrible business. You have a question for them?"

"Yes, that's correct." Bianka lowered herself into a chair.

"Then please, I will do my best. Hold my hands."

Podmore reached across the table, taking Bianka's hands. His hands felt like two dead trout waiting to be cooked into *trota arrosto alla salvia*. Podmore closed his eyes, bowed his head, inhaled deeply through clenched teeth, then loudly expelled the air in a short volley of gasps. Bianka shivered. The temperature dropped. Or, at least, it appeared to drop. After a minute or so, Podmore's head fell to one side and a bubble of drool formed at the corner of his mouth, then dangled there like string.

"Is anyone there?" Podmore's voice wavered.

No answer.

"If anyone is there, tap the table."

The table jolted and Podmore panted, spluttered, choked, then discharged a series of low guttural growling noises, followed by a high-pitched whistling. Then from his lips, a woman's voice.

"Bianka, is that you? This is your mother...oh the water is so cold...Bianka, you seem troubled by something...what is it? Speak to me, daughter, speak to me."

Bianka's heart sank. This wasn't her mother's voice.

"Speak to me, daughter, you are troubled. Speak to me."

Bianka sighed. "Yes, I am troubled. I'm troubled by where my mother learned to speak English, Mr. Podmore. She never spoke a word of English in her life, and she never called me Bianka. I was always her Piccolina. You're a charlatan."

A chill fell upon the Victorian sitting room on Argyle Street. The leaves on the potted plants withered, turned crisp, then fell onto the carpet. Frost settled on the picture frames. The men and women in the photographs, already frozen in time, now shivered and rubbed their hands together for warmth. Their teeth chattered with the cold. One by one they collapsed and died in their picture frames. Podmore tried to pull his hands away from Bianka's, but the petite Italian cook tightened her vice-like grip.

"You are a fraud, Mr. Podmore. You take advantage of vulnerable people, and I find that to be evil. I'm afraid that people like you are destined to rot for all eternity in hell. You have upset me, Mr. Podmore. I am very, very upset."

Podmore's metacarpals, carpals and phalanges crackled like sticks in a campfire. Bianka tightened her grip. It was as if she were crumbling crackers into a bowl of her homemade minestrone soup. Podmore tried to scream, but no noise escaped his lips. He was mute, his stifled cries for mercy clotting in his throat. He fixed his gaze upon Bianka.

His eyes pleaded with her to stop, but instead of the little Italian cook he found himself staring into the demonic eyes of Astaroth, twenty-ninth spirit of Satan and Crowned Prince of Hell. The garish red poppy wallpaper shredded itself into a million tiny pieces and floated like dust around the room, turning it into a hellish snow-globe. Bianka threw back her head and a six-foot reptilian tongue shot from her mouth, across the table, then down David Podmore's throat. It yanked out his lungs and splattered them against the wall, where they were consumed in a feeding frenzy by tiny pieces of carnivorous wallpaper. Podmore's lifeless body slumped forward onto the table, then slid to the floor. Flecks of wallpaper stripped the flesh from the corpse like piranha fish. Suddenly the door was flung open and Persephone ran into the room, to be halted by Bianka's razor-sharp tongue, as it whiplashed around the room and sliced off her head. A blizzard of wallpaper cleaned up the mess. All that was left were two bleached-white skeletons on the floor of a Victorian sitting room cluttered with dead plants, empty picture frames, and wallpaper with red poppies that bled to the touch.

Bianka explored the house, pocketing jewelry from Persephone's bedroom and a wad of cash, mostly bills with that ghastly Grant fellow on them, from a drawer in Podmore's desk. Bianka felt the shroud of gloom left by her parents' death lifted, leaving her light-headed and joyous. The spong popped the boil of pent-up emotions and Satan's pus burst out, killing everything in its path. Bianka checked her make-up in the hall mirror, applied more powder to her cheeks and a layer of lipstick. She left the house and strolled home down the lakefront. It was a beautiful day. The sun shining, the waters of the lake calm, families picnicking. Excited children sand-modeled, molding handfuls of wet sand into the shape of hats, cats, dogs and other animals. Boys playing playground ball and kickball, girls deep-water walking. There was also a watermelon grab.

The next morning a headline on the front page of the *Chicago Tribune* read: "Ghastly Murder on Argyle Street: Two Drained of Blood. Police looking for monster." The *Chicago Daily News* wrote: "Flesh Stripped from Bones: Ripper at large in Chicago."

EIGHT

The Clam sisters cast off the shackles of religion and the ritual of Sunday mass at Holy Name Cathedral. God had become a millstone around their necks, no, a straitjacket, or better: a Bien Jolie one-piece girdle and brassiere corset. Maude, Charlotte and Amelia were too busy hatching, flexing their wings, and fleeing mediocrity to bother with sanctified mumbo-jumbo. None of the Clam sisters entered Holy Name Cathedral ever again.

The Clam sisters' staff, Caitlin and Bianka, felt the spong's radiance on their cheeks, leading Caitlin to fellate a heavily-tattooed Chinese bodyguard and Bianka to rip out the innards and strip the flesh from a fraudulent clairvoyant.

After Sunday morning breakfast, a new gleaming black Chrysler Six pulled up outside Palourde Parlor. Charlotte climbed into the back seat with Lin Kwang, who carried a Thompson submachine gun under his long raincoat. The driver, a Chinaman wearing chauffeur's livery of jacket and breeches, headed south through downtown Chicago toward Chinatown. Soon after they left, Edward drove Maude to Oak Street Beach, where she set up her easel on the grass in the shade of a catalpa tree. Edward sat in the car reading the *Chicago Tribune*. Maude leaned back and compared her painting of the Drake Hotel to the hotel itself. It was a good likeness, but she hated both, the building and the painting. They were ugly. She angrily daubed splotches of blue paint over the canvas, then took it to the beach and laid it face down in the sand. She carried the painting back to her easel, hurriedly painted three rows of cave-like windows onto the gritty canvas, then stood back and admired her work.

"Edward! What do you think of my painting? It's finished."

Edward appraised the picture. "I think it's a very good likeness. A sandy cliff-face with caves in it. Obviously, it's inspired by Henry Blake Fuller's book *The Cliff-Dwellers*. It's perfect."

"Thank you. Now, I'm going to promenade along the beachfront awhile. You stay here and guard my painting, now that it's officially a work of art."

Maude laughed, slid on her sunglasses, unfurled her parasol and headed south on the grass verge. Edward stood near her stool, guarding the painting against art thieves. He stared out over Lake Michigan at a gaff-rigged topsail schooner sailing away. He could just make out the name, the *Adventurer*. Edward fought the urge to strip off his clothes, swim out and drag himself up on board, be a stowaway. Perhaps the *Adventurer* would take him through the Great Lakes and out to sea, away to a tropical paradise. Out the corner of his eye, he saw a man standing nearby, staring at him intently. He was clean-shaven, about thirty-five years of age, very dashing in his straw hat, worsted two-piece bathing suit with a top of horizontal college stripes, navy blue trunks, and canvas belt. The man approached him.

"I see you are an artist."

"No, no, no, I'm the chauffeur, my lady is the artist."

"I see, but I'm thinking that you yourself are a work of art."

"Oh!" Edward laughed, nervously.

"Here is my calling card. Are you busy tomorrow night?"

"No, I have the night off."

"Perfect. Shall we say seven o'clock? I have a proposition for you, a job offer."

The handsome gentleman turned and walked away. Edward watched until he disappeared into the crowds on the beach. Then he read the card: *Max Dorsey, 1255 W. Elmdale*.

"Max Dorsey, the film producer?" Edward checked the card again. What could Max Dorsey want with him?

NINE

The disappearance of David Podmore and his assistant Persephone Davidson baffled the Chicago Police Department. At first they suspected the two bleached-white skeletons to be their remains. However, witnesses had seen Podmore and Davidson earlier that morning: Podmore strolling in Lincoln Park with his long stride and silver-topped cane, and Davidson buying potatoes in the local grocery store. It would be nigh-impossible to murder, strip their skeletons of flesh, and bleach the bones in but a couple of hours.

So police focused on Podmore and Davidson as the killers of two unknown persons. The bleeding red poppy wallpaper doubled the mystery. There were other theories, that it was the work of vampires, werewolves, or a poltergeist. A Satanic cult was mentioned, space aliens, Mormons, philatelists even. Why General Superintendent Morgan A. Collins blamed psychotic stamp collectors is anyone's guess. The fingers of blame pointed in all directions.

Nobody suspected a petite Italian cook.

On Monday morning, Caitlin woke from a nightmare. Karl Marx wrote: "Die Religion…ist das Opium des Volkes," For some addicted to Christianity, coming off the God drug causes bad dreams and night sweats. In Caitlin's nightmare an aging priest in black and purple vestments stood at the altar of Holy Name Cathedral and repeated: "Áve María, grátia pléna, Dóminus técum. Benedícta tu in muliéribus, et benedíctus frúctus véntris túi, Iésus. Sáncta María, Máter Déi, óra pro nóbis peccatóribus, nunc et in hóra mórtis nóstrae. Ámen." Caitlin sat upright in bed, fearful of burning for all eternity in the fires of hell, but the fear evaporated when she found Lin Kwang lying next to her. She kissed the bodyguard's chest, then sank beneath the sheets to swallow the dragon. The scaly reptile struggled in her mouth for a while. Tense, throb, throb, a-throbbing, then exploding, just like the blue spong. When spent, Lin Kwang's fearsome dragon returned to its cave to sleep a while longer.

Meanwhile, Maude woke up to a revelation. She named her painting of the Drake Hotel "The Red Masque Snapped in Darkness by Centipedes." Surrealism arrived in Chicago through Maude's paintbrush via Oak Street Beach. She later threw the painting into the trash, repeating "Da-Da Da-Da Da-Da Da-Da Da-Da Da-Da Da-Da Da-Da Da-Da Da-Da Da-Da Da-Da Da-Da." Maude never painted again. She insisted that "not painting" was her gift to the art world.

AMELIA'S DATE WITH the anarchist Antonio Corigliani didn't end with a kiss on the doorstep, but lustily in her bedroom. Amelia first swam naked in the dark pools of Antonio's eyes, felt his soft hair on her cheek, tasted the sweat on his chest, then mounted him, riding him through the illusory stone pine forests of southern Italy. She stifled screams of unbridled joy as he slid his prick deep inside of her, again, and again, and again. In the throes of passion, neither of them noticed they were being watched. The blue spong, hidden behind a Tiffany lamp, throbbed gently with voyeuristic glee. It throb, throb, a-throbbed, then exploded with steel-blue light. Earlier in the evening, Antonio had arrived on the doorstep at Palourde Parlor clutching a single rose. He wore an ill-fitting suit, shirt unironed, and on his feet a pair of scuffed shoes, the soles breaking away. Amelia wore a flesh-tone-colored chiffon slip with an overdress of black lace and satin, black shoes and matching hose. The unlikely pair strolled half a block to the Gray Cottage, where a motley collection of bohemians gathered. Antonio introduced Amelia to his friends, Lizzie Ball, a bibulous hobo and Marxist intellectual with a shock of red hair and cocaine eyes, and Aldeban, an undernourished hermaphrodite violinist.

Aldeban told Amelia, "Don't call me a lady, and don't call me a man. Call me Aldeban." The hermaphrodite lifted their violin and played a brief sad refrain.

A group of agitated men hunched over a table smoking cigarettes, drinking strong coffee, and arguing over the merits of James Joyce's *Ulysses.*

"I bought my copy in Paris from Sylvia Beach herself at her bookstore, Shakespeare and Company on 8 rue Dupuytren." The man drained his cigarette and stubbed it into an ashtray.

"The location of the purchase is immaterial," his friend scoffed, banging his fist on the table. "The book is nothing more than the ass-droppings of a lunatic."

A stout middle-aged woman named Sam, who wore a man's suit, shirt with collar and tie, and a lavender derby, laughed and slid her arm about her companion's waist, kissing the young woman on the cheek.

"This is my lady friend! This is the girl of my dreams. My bride to be."

A hush fell over the gathering when a man in his early forties with wild eyes, a bushy mustache, and unkempt hair, stepped onto a small stage clutching a book.

"My name is Konrad Bercovici, and I am from the country of Romania, though I speak several languages, English…as you can hear…Greek, Romanian, French and German, and I can swear in Russian. *Pokazhi pizdu detka*… I should be arrested for saying that."

"What does it mean?" The question came from a young sailor.

"I am inviting you to drop your trousers and reveal to us your vagina."

The crowd roared. One man leapt to his feet, put his arm around Sam's shoulders and shouted. "I will only show it to my wife, she is here… HE is my darling! SHE is my husband!"

Sam pushed him away. "I am most certainly not your husband! If I were your husband, or your wife, you would have been poisoned by now. I would have fed you arsenic."

The crowd roared again, but when Bercovici opened his book, a silence fell over the Gray Cottage. He read passages from *Love and the Gypsy.* Amelia was rapt. It was as if she were sitting on a rock listening to Jesus Christ's Sermon on the Mount. Every word Bercovici uttered was a precious drop of insight trickling into the hitherto empty vessel of her life.

Antonio slid his arm around Amelia's waist. "So what do you think of the Gray Cottage?"

"I feel like you've opened my cage and let me out. Like I have awoken to find the straps of bondage removed."

Antonio laughed. "Not me. I've done nothing but bring you here. It's because Bercovici is communicating with you and where there is real communication between people there is no need for states, religions or governments."

Bercovici left the stage to thunderous applause. When the crowd settled again, Aldeban leapt onto the dais, lifted his violin and played a Russian gypsy folk song, while Lizzie Ball danced between the tables singing.

"The cattails whispered,
the trees wagged their branches
And the night was gloomy and dark
But two lovers walked together until morning
Why are you crying, my love?
He asked her noticing the tears on her cheeks
Maybe you don't love me anymore?

"Oh my darling I love you very much
And I cry because I don't want to part with you
Because I feel that I can't live without you.

"The cattails whispered,
the trees wagged their branches
And the night was gloomy and dark
But two lovers walked together until morning."

CAITLIN WAITED FOR the Clam sisters to return home from their adventures. Maude arrived at the witching hour, giggling, arm in arm with Minnie Fish-Griffin. They'd spent a raucous evening in the Green Mask, entertained by performers from a traveling vaudeville show. The Greenwich Village Follies at the Schubert Garrick was advertised in the *Chicago Tribune* as: "The Bohemians Inc. Present a Panorama of Silken Tights and Subtle Lights and Swift and Comic Escapades." After the show, the performers tumbled into the Green Mask. A male impersonator, wearing a Jolly Jack Tar sailor's suit, stood up and sang "I Wonder Who's Kissing Her Now" while Minnie tickled the ivories. Charlotte arrived at Palourde Parlor soon afterwards with her lover Chin Wing, his two bodyguards Chan Yan-tak and Yi Yin, and Lin Kwang. Amelia arrived just after midnight with a crapulent Antonio Corigliani. He could barely stand up, singing "The Internationale" at the top of his lungs.

"Compagni avanti il gran partito
Noi siamo dei lavorator.
Rosso un fiore in petto c'è fiorito.
Una fede c'è nata in cor.
Noi non siampo più nell'officina.
Entro terra ai campi al mar

La plebe sempre all'opra china
Senza ideale in cui sperar.

Su lottiamo! L'ideale
Nostro alfine sarà
L'Internazionale
Futura umanità."

Caitlin escorted the three Chinese bodyguards downstairs and fellated each in turn. After swallowing three Hip Sing dragons, Caitlin curled up in bed with Lin Kwang. He held her in his tattooed arms. She melted. Rumors of Caitlin's skills in the art of fellatio spread rapidly amongst Hip Sing henchmen and gangsters in Chinatown. She slipped thirty dollars into her purse for her Rainy Day Fund. The spong hovered in the corridor outside, throb, throb, a-throbbing, then sending out shards of steel-blue light.

EARLY MORNINGS BELOW stairs at Palourde Parlor were a hectic affair with Bianka baking muffins, stirring scrambled eggs, and frying bacon on the griddle, Celie and Clotilda tending to the laundry and Caitlin helping out where needed. Today was busier than usual because of the Clam sisters' overnight guests, Chin Wing, Minnie Fish-Griffin, Antonio Corigliani, and the three Hip Sing bodyguards, Lin Kwang, Chan Yan-tak and Yi Yin.

Bianka muttered under her breath. "How am I supposed to know what Chinamen eat for breakfast?"

"Zongzi, they're rice dumplings wrapped in bamboo leaves and steamed." Caitlin sailed through the kitchen.

"Where did you learn about Chinese cuisine?"

"I know a little bit about a lot of things."

The morning routine was also disrupted by the disappearance of Clotilda Schulze, the parlor maid. Her bed had not been slept in.

"It's not like her." Bianka cracked eggs into a bowl. "She's always up early. Sometimes she's up before me."

"The last time I saw Clotilda was yesterday morning, she was helping us with breakfast." Caitlin washed her hands and dried them on a towel. "I remember her pulling a tray of muffins out of the oven, then carrying a laundry basket upstairs."

Celie joined them. "She went to church. I saw her leave. She was wearing her church hat and her church shoes and her church face."

"Did she have any family or friends? I never asked her about it. In fact, she was such a quiet little thing that I hardly noticed she was here." Caitlin filled a teapot with boiling water. "I'll tell the Clam sisters, they'll know what to do."

Celie braced herself. "There's something else you need to tell them. You need to tell them I have a new job. I'm moving on. I'll stay until the end of next week."

Bianka dropped a knife into the sink. "Where are you going?"

"I'll be working at Miss Sadie's Galloping Stallion Riding Stables for Gentlemen with Equestrian Taste."

"Where have I heard that name before?" In truth, Caitlin knew exactly where she'd heard the name before.

"Miss Maude and Miss Minnie were arrested in the nightclub with one of the stable workers there. Nelly. I will be breaking-in and riding men who like to pretend they're horses. Miss Sadie said I'm a natural with a riding crop. Apparently I have a determined gleam in my eye and can be ruthless when necessary."

The blue spong hovered above Celie and throbbed gently.

"I think you're right to get other employment. We should all be looking to move on from here." Caitlin arranged blueberry muffins on a platter. "In fact, I've also been offered an opportunity to better myself, in Chinatown."

Bianka dropped another knife in the sink. "Doing what?"

"Never you mind."

While the women busied themselves in the kitchen, the staff dining room next door was heady with the musk of masculinity. Edward, who lived in the coach house above the garage, arrived for breakfast to find three Chinamen sitting at the dining table. Above their heads the spong throb, throb, throbbed, then exploded, sending out gunmetal-blue light. Edward bathed in the pool of virility. Even when Richard Clam was alive Palourde Parlor had been a woman's house. Amelia, Maude, Charlotte, and their mother Sarah ruled the roost. Sometimes it seemed like Richard was pushed out by the sheer force of menstrual magic conjured up by this coven of witches. Richard saw himself as a well-oiled machine, with Edward, his wife and three daughters, along with the staff, the cogs and wheels that moved him forward. His life was a chugging mass of grease and gears. He was only happy when Edward was deep inside of him, greased and pumping him up. It was when the machine broke down that he and his wife jumped from a station platform into an oncoming train. His death left Edward the only male living at Palourde Parlor. Now there were three Hip Sing bodyguards there, all wearing Colt .38 revolvers, and, propped up against the wall, three Thompson submachine guns. Each of the Chinamen wore the traditional queue hairstyle, shorn at the forehead, a pigtail hanging down the back.

The queue had been compulsory, until two years earlier, when Puyi, the Emperor of China, cut his hair, freeing up a nation of men to reach for the scissors. However, many in Chicago's Chinatown held onto the old traditions.

The blue spong circled the room twice, then descended slowly onto Lin Kwang's shoulder.

"The spong likes you."

Edward sat with the bodyguards. He fought the urge to reach out and touch Lin Kwang's tattoos to see if they were real.

"Oh, the spong and I are old friends. We have known each other my whole life…and also in my life before this life…and the life before that…and my many lives before that."

Yi Yin and Chan Yan-tak nodded in agreement.

They were interrupted by a triple-knock at the door. Edward answered it to find a tall thin woman in her mid-sixties wearing a lopsided woolen cap, struggling with two large bags. "I'm Jenny, I've brought clean clothes for Miss Minnie Fish-Griffin. She is here, isn't she?"

"I don't know." Edward shrugged his shoulders.

"I can't keep up with her. One minute she's here, then she's there, and then who knows where! She's a very difficult person to look after. Overindulged if you ask me. Of course, nobody has ever asked me. But in the unlikely event that I was asked for an opinion, I would say that Miss Minnie Fish-Griffin is overindulged."

"You had better come in." Edward lifted her bags into the dining room.

Charles Fish-Griffin owned a chain of department stores, though his daughter Minnie eschewed the trappings of wealth and opted for a bohemian lifestyle. She rented her own apartment, paid for with money earned from her piano recitals. However, one vestige of her old life was Jenny, her childhood nanny, still hired by her parents to look after their youngest daughter. Minnie was adept at losing Jenny in a crowd. Many times Minnie Fish-Griffin darted down alleys or out the back door of a store to lose her old nanny.

"I know she was out with Miss Maude Clam last night. So when she didn't come home, I guessed she was here."

"She is here!" Caitlin called from the kitchen. "I'll get Celie to take the bags up to her. Sit down. Would you like coffee or tea?"

"Coffee."

Jenny sat at the table. "Oh, three Chinamen! How exciting! What's that?" Jenny pointed at the spinning orb.

Edward shrugged. "It's a blue spong."

"But what is it?"

"I have no idea."

Again they were interrupted by a knock at the door. This time Edward found two women in their late twenties, wearing identical red dresses with white spots, white collars, short sleeves cuffed at the elbow, dropped waists, and on their heads, the same cloche hat. Identical twins.

"Good morning, I'm Kamilla."

"I'm Katharina."

"Baum." The twins said together.

"Both called Baum." Kamilla brushed imaginary dust from her shoulder. "We're related to L. Frank Baum who wrote *The Wonderful Wizard of Oz*, although he wasn't a Lutheran."

"Not a Lutheran at all. He was Episcopalian."

"Who became a Theosophist, whatever that is, we're not sure, are we, Katharina?"

"No, we're not."

"Anyway, we're not here to discuss L. Frank Baum. We've come about Clotilda Schulze."

"You'd better come in." Edward waved them into the crowded dining room.

"So what's happening here?" Caitlin breezed in from the kitchen. "It's beginning to look like a railway station. When's the next train leaving? Choo-choo!"

Edward returned to the table. "Caitlin, they've come about Clotilda."

"What about Clotilda? We know she's missing. Do you know where she is?"

"She disappeared." Kamilla blurted out.

"Before our very eyes." Katharina finished her sister's sentence. It was impossible for either Kamilla or Katharina Baum to finish a sentence without the other's help.

"Can somebody explain what's going on?" Caitlin joined the others at the dining table.

"We're from Holy Trinity Lutheran Church." Kamilla began the sentence. "We've come to tell you that Clotilda... This is difficult. We were all in the church yesterday morning, when Clotilda walked in...she was late. Well, she was walking down the aisle to her seat. She got to the front of the church and she—"

"She disappeared." Katharina finished the sentence.

Caitlin leaned back in her chair. "What do you mean by 'disappear'?"

Kamilla began, "What she means is that Clotilda completely disappeared."

"In the church, into thin air," Katharina finished.

The blue spong hovered three feet above the twins.

"What is that?" Kamilla pointed at the glowing orb.

"Oh, that's just Miss Charlotte's spong. So Clotilda disappeared in the church, did she?" Caitlin was intrigued. She had read Sir Arthur Conan Doyle's Sherlock Holmes adventure *The Valley of Fear.* She was gripped. Mysteries drove her crazy.

"Before our very eyes," Katharina began.

"One minute she was there, then…poof! She was gone, and everyone in the congregation saw it," Kamilla finished.

"Have you told the police?"

"Told them what?" Kamilla began. "That we saw someone disappear into thin air? How do you think that would sound?"

"They would take us away to the asylum in restraints. We would be locked up," Katharina finished.

"I think she was taken by Jesus." Kamilla smiled. "It's the only rational explanation."

Everybody in the room waited for Katharina to finish the sentence. She was silent.

In the kitchen, Bianka screamed. Pigtails flying, Lin Kwang, Yi Yin and Chan Yan-tak burst into the kitchen, their revolvers drawn and aimed at a young man. He was wearing loose-fitting pants held up by purple suspenders. He was also barefoot and naked to the waist. The man's hands shot up in the air. "*Mi chiamo Antonio Corigliani. Sono un anarchista e sono qui per aiutarti a preparare colazione.* I am only here to help. I am Amelia's guest, but I must help you prepare breakfast, as I cannot benefit from, or aid in any way, your slavery."

Caitlin stepped forward. "Young man, if you help us with breakfast then you are taking away our jobs. Then how would you have helped us? We're paid to do this. You would be offering free labor to the 'ruling class' upstairs. I believe that would make *you* the slave and banish us into unemployment. You assume that because I'm a mere housekeeper, an Irish woman, that I have never read a book on this subject. I have read Karl Marx' *Das Kapital* cover to cover."

Caitlin chest puffed up. She had managed to out-Marx an anarchist. Antonio reddened, bowed respectfully, and retreated upstairs.

"Well done, Caitlin." Edward clapped his hands. "You certainly sent him packing with his tail between his legs."

"What happened to her?" Caitlin pointed to Katharina prostrate on the floor.

"She fainted. She's never seen a man's nipples before. I'm not sure that she even knew they had nipples." Kamilla reddened.

"Of course men have nipples. How can she not know that? That was Amelia's young gentlemen friend. Likes to think of himself as a radical and a troublemaker."

THAT AFTERNOON EDWARD boarded the train to the Thorndale elevated stop. He skipped down the stairs, turned right, then right again at the Jewish delicatessen. He peered in the window at the trays of babka, hamantashen, and lekach. Jewish food fascinated him but he had yet to try it. He crossed the street and stopped outside a six-flat apartment building. It was a warm evening and lovers strolled by arm in arm. Soon dusk would fall and the night sky be pinpricked by the glow of lightning bugs. Bareheaded, his shirtsleeves rolled up above the elbow, Edward carried a light jacket over his arm. He checked the card again. Max Dorsey, 1255 W. Elmdale. He pressed the doorbell. Dorsey answered it, but instead of inviting the chauffeur inside, he motioned him toward a parked car.

"Come on, it's only a short drive."

"Where are we going?"

"Oh, I'm sorry, didn't I explain? I'm taking you for a screen test. Let's see if the camera likes you as much as I do."

TEN

KATHARINA BAUM LAY on the bed in Clotilda's room, her sister pressing a damp cloth to her brow. Katharina was still shaken.

"I didn't know that men had nipples." Katharina gasped for air.

"It's a well-known fact."

"But what are they for? I don't understand why they have them. Nipples are for feeding babies. Men don't feed babies."

"I don't think anybody knows why men have nipples but they do. Perhaps you should pray and ask God. I suspect he's the one who gave men nipples in the first place. His design…he must have had something in mind for them. Perhaps they're decorative."

Katharina shuddered. "Have you noticed how cold Clotilda's room is? Not just the temperature. There's no warmth here, no photographs, no personal items. Just soap, a hairbrush, a few clothes. It's as if she didn't exist at all."

"Perhaps Clotilda is a ghost."

"That would certainly explain her disappearance. This is a very sad room."

"Perhaps we should put up some pictures, a vase of flowers, there on the chest of drawers." Kamilla jabbed her finger in the air. "A few books on that shelf might lift the sadness away. We could make it more comfortable for Clotilda's return."

The spong hovered over the bed and throb, throb, a-throbbed, until it exploded until nothing much was left but a few blue fizzles.

"Is that thing following us?" Katharina studied the blue spong.

"I think it is."

BREAKFAST WAS A busier affair than usual, with the addition of Minnie Fish-Griffin, Chin Wing and Antonio Corigliani, the Clam sisters' lovers.

"The scrambled eggs are delicious." Minnie broke the awkward silence. "I detect cream in them and dill, perhaps. Who is your cook?"

"Her name is Bianka." Antonio helped himself to a bowl of oatmeal. "I offered to help her in the kitchen this morning, but my good intentions were spurned. I was put in my place. Your housekeeper is a very intelligent woman, perhaps she is even a revolutionary."

"Caitlin, a revolutionary." Maude doubled over with laughter "I think that's most unlikely."

Caitlin entered with the menu for dinner. She handed it to Charlotte.

"Oh, I won't be here for dinner tonight. What about you, Maude?"

"I won't be here either."

"Amelia?"

"Not me, I'm out this evening."

Caitlin took back the menu, tore it in half and slid the pieces into her pocket. "There have been some developments downstairs, Miss Charlotte. Can I speak to you after breakfast?"

"Speak to me now, I'm leaving after breakfast."

CAITLIN REPEATED KATHARINA and Kamilla Baum's story about Clotilda's mysterious disappearance, how Jenny arrived with Minnie's bags and about Celie's new position at Miss Sadie's Galloping Stallion Riding Stables for Gentlemen with Equestrian Taste.

"What a coincidence about Miss Sadie's Stables. After we met Nelly the prostitute at the police station." Maude noticed the blue spong hovering above Amelia's head, throb, throb, a-throbbing.

Charlotte changed the subject. "What are we going to do about Clotilda? People don't disappear walking up the aisle of a church. It just doesn't happen."

"It sounds intriguing. I can cancel my plans and visit the church." Amelia wiped the corners of her mouth with a napkin.

"I'll come with you." Antonio held Amelia's hand.

Charlotte thought for a moment. "Who are these Baum sisters? They seem like an odd pair to me."

"They're twins. Related to L. Frank Baum, *The Wonderful Wizard of Oz* author." Caitlin hesitated. "They're currently recovering in Clotilda's room."

"Recovering from what?"

"One of them passed out cold when she saw Mr. Corigliani's

nipples earlier this morning."

"So you're telling me that Mr. Corigliani showed his nipples to the kitchen staff this morning."

"Yes, Miss Charlotte." Caitlin stared at her shoes, avoiding Antonio's gaze.

"How odd. How very odd, indeed. What is it about your nipples that is so frightening, Mr. Corigliani?"

"I do not know, Miss Charlotte. Perhaps I have the nipples of a vampire."

"Do vampires have nipples?" Maude laughed. She wondered if vampire matrons nursed small infants with fangs. It all made her quiver.

While the conversation continued on the subject of vampire nipples, the spong hovered over the breakfast table, throb, throb, a-throbbing. Of course, it burst.

After breakfast, Amelia and Antonio spoke to the Baum twins before setting out for the church.

"Martin Luther was an interesting man. He split from the Roman Catholic Church and launched the Protestant Reformation after posting his Ninety-Five Theses on the door of the Castle Church of Wittenberg. In many ways he was a revolutionary."

"Who offered more opium to the people." Amelia was dismissive.

"You are right, of course, Lutheranism is nothing but shit of a different color." The couple turned the corner into Oak Street. "Mikhail Bakunin said, 'People go to church for the same reasons they go to a tavern, to stupefy themselves, to forget their misery, to imagine themselves, for a few minutes anyway, free and happy.'"

"Yes, I agree with Bakunin. There is no God. It's all nonsense."

The two revolutionaries skipped down the street arm in arm like children. A music box played in their heads. Every skip took Amelia further way from mediocrity. Further away from Palourde Parlor. Amelia stopped to examine her shadow lying across a patch of grass. There were two nubs on its back, the beginning of wings. She felt the scratchy feathers.

Holy Trinity Church was a Gothic edifice, made from Wisconsin Lannon stone, built to withstand the harshest of Chicago winters. The stained-glass windows depicted the apostles, some bearded and pious, others clean-shaven and cherubic. Above the altar, a triptych showed Christ cradling a babe in his arms. At his feet a quartet of languid sheep chewed grass. Amelia and Antonio pushed through the hubbub of reporters and police gathered outside the church.

Inside, the pastor's head was visible above a huddle of anxious parishioners.

"Good morning, my name is Amelia Clam." Amelia elbowed her way through the crowd. "Clotilda works for me. This morning I spoke to two of your congregants, the Baum sisters, and a very strange tale they had to tell."

"Yes, I apologize for all this commotion. Come with me, let's find some peace and quiet." The pastor guided them through a side door, down a dimly lit corridor and into a neat office. "I'm afraid someone has called the police and the newspapers. I am the Rev. Eric Gustavson by the way. What did the Baums tell you?" He closed the door and sat behind his desk. "Please sit down."

"They said Clotilda vanished in the church. She has worked for my family for some years."

"Yes, the church was almost full at the time. Clotilda walked in the door, the Baum sisters were sitting about halfway down, and I, of course, was standing at the altar. Clotilda walked down the aisle and suddenly disappeared into thin air. It was as if she walked into...nothingness. Some people are saying it's a miracle. That she was taken by Jesus."

"Or it could have been a conjuring trick. Like Houdini jumping into a river with his hands cuffed to his feet and climbing out of the water ten minutes later. Or the Chinese Water Torture Cell Trick, where he is shackled and submerged in a tank of water and miraculously escapes."

"But what would be the purpose of that? Clotilda was not a magician, she was a maid. She was a rather timid little thing, not given to theatrical stunts. It's a mystery."

Amelia and Antonio left the church none the wiser.

WALKING BACK TO Chestnut Street, Amelia and Antonio stopped for coffee and a slice of cake at the Petite Gourmet Café in Towertown. The café was a magnet for writers like Henry Blake Fuller, Witter Bynner, and the "It Girl" of poetry, Edna St. Vincent Millay, a trio of wordsmiths who haunted the dilapidated buildings in this maze of tiny streets. Some of the rickety structures had staircases leading up to little theaters, or art studios in garrets. In the back alleys, stables were now bookstores run by characters like Dada Diana, a woman who wore spoon earrings and preached the philosophy of free love and paganism, and Red Mickey, a hobo from Virginia, the spitting image of Leon Trotsky. Towertown was a crucible for new ideas, inhabited by frauds, phonies, and the real thing. A hustling, bustling

Sapphic bohemia, where feminine men skipped lightly, their wrists limp and jangling with slave bracelets, and masculine women smoked stogies and swung silver-topped canes. The graffiti on the walls of Towertown read "Tzara Tzara Tzara," a mantra and homage to the author of the *Seven Dada Manifestos* and *Lampisteries.* In the center of Towertown sat the Clams' mansion, an island of affluence in a vast sea of poverty. Though, in reality, it was the reverse, because Palourde Parlor suffered a paucity of dreams and a crippling poverty of the imagination, while the grubby and unkempt streets surrounding it were rich with new ideas and affluent with fanciful notions.

Amelia opened the door to Palourde Parlor to hear music coming from upstairs. When her parents were alive there had been parties and dances in the ballroom. Richard and Sarah Clam were regulars on the Society page of the *Chicago Tribune*. August 15, 1915 read: "Mr. and Mrs. Richard Clam will be at home this afternoon and evening at Palourde Parlor. Mrs. S. Wright Golding, Mrs. Charles E. Latimer, Miss Grace Golding, and Miss Florence Latimer will assist in receiving." And in the April 19, 1917 issue: "Mrs. Sarah Clam, Amelia Clam, Charlotte Clam, and Maude Clam, have returned from California." Amelia paused in the hallway, closed her eyes and listened as the tumbling notes of Beethoven's "Für Elise" floated down the stairwell like confetti. She squeezed Antonio's hand. "I haven't heard music in this house since my parents passed away." Antonio pulled her close and kissed her on the lips. A kiss interrupted by a stout middle-aged man in a checkered suit tripping down the stairs carrying a leather bag bearing the name P.A. Starck Piano Co. He dashed past the embracing couple, heading for the door. "I'm the piano tuner, in case you were wondering." Then he was gone, leaving only the faint smell of sarcasm, mixed with Palmolive shaving cream.

Amelia ran up the stairs to the music room, where Minnie Fish-Griffin sat at the piano, her fingers fluttering over the keys like drunken butterflies. Maude stood nearby, barely recognizable in a pair of gray flannel trousers, a blue tattersall waistcoat, gray madras shirt, blue foulard tie and hair pinned up under a straw hat with a blue and gray band. Above her lip rested a painted rakish mustache, slightly turned up at the tips. The Baum sisters sat on a sofa.

Maude waved to Amelia. "Come and join us, we're rehearsing."

"Rehearsing for what?"

"Minnie and I are starting a vaudeville act."

"Then we must be your audience." Antonio sat between the Baum sisters on the sofa. "And to you, Miss Katharina, I must apologize. I didn't mean to frighten you this morning with my nipples. At home

I wear no clothes at all. I walk around the house as nature intended me to be. It's in my character to be free from all restrictions."

"Oh, really!" Katharina reddened. "I was taken by surprise, that's all. We won't mention it again. Ever again." Katharina tried to cast Antonio's nipples from her mind. She failed miserably. Katharina could not unsee Antonio's nipples.

Minnie straightened. She flexed her fingers and began to play. Maude leaned on the piano in what she perceived as a most masculine fashion.

"Will you love me in December as you do in May?
Will you love me in the good old-fashioned way?
When my hair has all turned gray,
Will you kiss me then and say,
That you love me in December as you do in May?"

When the song ended, Maude bowed to her audience. Amelia, Antonio and the Baum twins applauded enthusiastically, and the blue spong throbbed and throbbed, then exploded with light. Charlotte and Chin Wing joined the group. "We were listening outside on the landing, we didn't want to disturb you. Please continue."

Chin Wing offered a smile. "Your voice is very beautiful. You make a very convincing man."

"Sing another one." Amelia clapped her hands.

"I only know one other song. It's called 'I Wonder Who's Kissing Her Now.'"

Maude could not deny the lyrics.

Meanwhile, downstairs Caitlin knelt on a cushion with Lin Kwang, Chan Yan-tak and Yi Yin standing before her with their pants and underthings crumpled around their ankles. She swallowed their tattooed dragons one by one until they spat fire. The Hip Sing bodyguards were waiting to escort Chin Wing and Charlotte back to Chinatown. The tong war between the Hip Sing and On Leong had intensified after three of Chin Wing's men were gunned down in the street. The killings left a pall of unease over Chinatown, danger lurking in the shadows and alleyways. The funeral of the young men was set for tomorrow and Chin Wing was to lead the procession.

As the dragons slept, the three bodyguards each left a ten dollar bill on the nightstand. Caitlin slid the money into her purse. Later she took the bills to the Lake Shore Trust and Savings Bank to add to her Rainy Day Fund.

Outside, an ominous dark cloud moved over Lake Michigan and it drizzled with rain.

ELEVEN

THE MAGNETIC PULL of the blue spong proved irresistible to Kamilla and Katharina Baum, who took up residence in Clotilda's room at Palourde Parlor. The Baums lived with their parents who, if truth was told, didn't like them very much. Sidney and Dottie Baum viewed the twins as a blockage in their lives, a stumbling block, grit in their eye, a fly in their soup. After their birth, Dottie Baum took one look at the cherubic pair and vowed never to open her legs for her husband again. She didn't. The elder Baums were not parental. The twins had been a terrible accident, the result of a lapse of judgment while visiting the Sistine Chapel in Rome. The exquisite beauty of Michelangelo's ceiling and the sight of God reaching out to give life to a naked Adam led to Sidney and Dottie Baum finding a quiet corner in the Apostolic Palace. Their canoodling and wild fumbling led to the birth of twin girls nine months later. The story was often aired at parties or family get-togethers. Parenting was not for them. They were adventurers. Not in the slightest bit mediocre. However, their offspring were as dull as dishwater, apples that fell a long, long, long way way from the tree.

Though attractive in a China-doll way, the twins were not the marrying kind. They were already "married" to each other. The bond between the two sisters was stronger than that between a man and wife, wife and wife, or husband and husband. The Baum twins finished each other's sentences, wore the same clothes, had the same wart in the same place, and led the same life of utter mediocrity. The only thing that separated the Baum twins was an invisible mirror in which they admired themselves and each other. If a miracle occurred and they married, it would be to someone as unexceptional as them. If they bore children, they would smother them in their cribs with mediocrity. The Baum twins had nothing in their lives except Lutheranism and a joint collection of "interesting" buttons.

Jenny, Minnie Fish-Griffin's nanny, also felt the magnetic pull of the blue spong. She found a fold-out cot and set it up in a cupboard under the stairs, where she lay, shut the door, and hid in the darkness. It reminded her of her childhood in South Carolina when she hid from her father and the other Klansmen on horseback, riding to the colored side of town. Then, the following day, hearing whispers of a lynching. Hers was an angry childhood, filled with fire and brimstone and the smell of charred corpses. Then, after a chance meeting with a hobo, she jumped the rails and rode north to Chicago. That was over thirty-five years ago. However, jumping the rails was her last act of rebellion. She soon fell into the subservient role of nanny for several families, ending up with the Fish-Griffins, looking after their only child, Minnie. A job she kept until the free-spirited girl left her father's mansion and struck out on her own. Even then, Jenny continued in the role of nanny, following Minnie like a dog, always a few steps behind her.

THE CLAM SISTERS didn't notice the squatters at Palourde Parlor. They were oblivious, too busy with their respective flights from mediocrity. In a new development, the shadows cast by Charlotte, Maude and Amelia now had nubs of wings on their backs. Scratchy feathers. While Minnie and Maud rehearsed their vaudeville act in the music room, and Caitlin fellated Chinamen below stairs, Edward spent the afternoon nude in bed with Max Dorsey, the film producer. After finding love while Dorsey spilt his seed inside of Edward, they shared a cigarette and blew smoke rings into the hot sweaty air.

"The Essanay studios here in Chicago are a thing of the past." The glow of orgasm over, Max returned to business. "Gloria Swanson has gone, Charlie Chaplin, Wallace Beery, all gone to the West Coast. It's the weather here in Chicago. It's terrible for making movies. We'll be leaving in two weeks by train, to Hollywood in Los Angeles." Max slipped into his dressing gown.

"For what?"

"You'll be making a movie with femme-fatale vamp Nita Naldi called *Grave Encounters*. You'll be playing her love interest and victim. Do you know her work?"

"I saw her in *The Man from Beyond*."

"Well, don't get too excited, she's an Irish girl from New York

City and as dumb as dumb can be. They're also looking for handsome men to appear in *Riders of the Purple Sage* from the novel by Zane Grey. Can you ride a horse?"

"No."

"Horse-riding lessons start tomorrow, and acting lessons too."

Edward had never considered riding a horse before. Many a man; he wondered if riding men would make horseback riding a breeze. And as far as acting, well, he had told many a gent he was in love when he wasn't. Love was essential to foreplay, but after the sheets were damp, love paled next to a good bath.

"But what about my job? I haven't told the Clams I'm leaving."

"You better tell them, then. I'll be sending a car for you early tomorrow afternoon. You'll be moving into my spare room."

"But—"

"No buts." Max disappeared into the kitchen. "And you need to shave off the mustache. Up against Nita Naldi you need to look lovelorn and pathetic, not shiftier and greasier than she is."

Edward closed his eyes and imagined himself on the big screen opposite Nita Naldi, but all he could see was himself in the Vilma Bánky role in *The Son of the Sheik* being forced to submit to the dark passionate desires of Rudolph Valentino. Edward felt the nubs on the back of his shadow growing into feathers. Soon his shadow would be the shadow of a hawk, to aid his flight from mediocrity. At Palourde Parlor the blue spong, throb, throb, a-throbbed, and then exploded. Light spilt everywhere, soaking the bed sheets.

In the early hours of the morning, Caitlin woke. She heard noises. She struggled into her nightgown and crept upstairs to the hallway. It was empty, but she heard conspiratorial whispers on the landing above her head.

"Is there anybody up there?"

"Only me." Amelia's head poked over the bannisters. "Nothing to be bothered about. Go back to bed."

Caitlin sensed another presence, a woman judging by a tattered scarf on the floor in the hallway. She picked it up gingerly. It smelt of cigarettes and liquor. She hung it on a hat stand and returned to bed, where she cuddled up to the warm body of Kwang with his dragon tattoos and nipples like dried goji berries.

Maude and Minnie arrived first at the breakfast table.

"What are these?" Maude picked up a box of cereal.

"They're new, they're called Wheaties, purported to be the 'Breakfast of Champions.'" Minnie shook open the newspaper. "Put them in a bowl, pour milk over them and add sugar. It's simple. Maude, have you seen this? Charles W. Leggett, chief of the Evanston police department, has been shot and killed."

"Oh my goodness! How dreadful. Has anyone been arrested?"

"I don't think so. Oh, and look at this: there's been another mysterious death of a clairvoyant, a Miss Betsy Carswell. Only a skeleton remained. It's the same as that strange murder last week, two skeletons that time. The same thing with the wallpaper too…it bleeds to the touch. They think it's the same killer."

"'The Skeleton and the Bleeding Wallpaper,' sounds like a story by Edgar Allen Poe. I'm getting chills down my spine just thinking about it."

Charlotte entered with Chin Wing at her side. "Chills about what?"

"In the newspaper." Minnie pointed to the article on the front page. "Another clairvoyant has been murdered in a most dastardly way. She was stripped of all her flesh and in the room where she was killed the wallpaper bled to the touch."

"It's a wicked sorcery." Chin Wing scowled. "The potent power of dark magic is everywhere."

The spong hovered near a Tiffany floor lamp and throbbed, throbbed, a-throbbed, before exploding.

A bedraggled Amelia and Antonio stood in the doorway. They looked like two dog toys dragged through the dirt. With them was a scruffy hobo woman, her clothes torn. She was limping. She was also cut and bruised about the face, arms, and neck. Antonio eased the woman into a chair and filled her plate with bacon and scrambled eggs.

"Thank you." The woman struggled to pick up a fork.

Charlotte broke the silence. "Well, aren't you going to introduce us to your friend? She seems to be in some distress. Should we call a doctor?"

"No," Amelia snapped, then glanced nervously at Charlotte. "This is Lizzie Ball. She doesn't need a doctor."

"I disagree…the poor woman is in a terrible state."

"I think we need some kind of explanation." Maude shuffled in her chair. "This woman has obviously been involved in an altercation. Perhaps she walked into a streetcar, or gone three rounds with Harry Greb, the pugilist. Something has happened to her."

Amelia flushed. "I'm afraid I'm going to have to ask all of you for your discretion and help. We have a problem."

"A serious problem." Antonio held Lizzie's hand as she tried to eat. "We need to get Lizzie out of Chicago. Out of the country, in fact."

"Why?" A spoonful of raspberries froze mid-air between Maude's fingertips. "What happened?"

"There's been an incident. A terrible incident."

Minnie Fish-Griffin held up the newspaper with the headline "Police Chief Dead." "Is it anything to do with this? It says here that the police are looking for a hobo woman, a Marxist revolutionary with bad breath and unreliable footwear."

Amelia sighed. "I can explain everything. You see, it was all a mistake. Antonio and I were at a labor protest supporting strikers, and the police tried to arrest Lizzie. Two policemen pushed her to the ground, and somehow the police chief was shot and killed."

"Somehow?" Charlotte went rigid. "People don't *somehow* get shot. Usually *someone* shoots them. Anyway, what do the misfortunes of this woman have to do with us? Why are we about to become entangled in this web of intrigue?"

"They think it was Lizzie who shot the police chief."

"And it wasn't her?"

"No, it was me who shot him."

The room fell silent. A full minute passed. Charlotte dabbed the corners of her mouth with a napkin. "Why would the Evanston Chief of Police be at a protest? Don't they sit in offices and order other people about? You don't expect to see them on the front lines, do you?"

"Isn't it immaterial why he was there?" Minnie folded the newspaper and placed it on the table. "The point is that Amelia has got herself into a jam."

Amelia wiped tears from her eyes. "All I know is that two policemen were struggling with Lizzie and I took one their guns and fired it. I shot the Chief of Police. Then the strikers lunged forward and Lizzie was dragged from the policemen's clutches, bundled into a car and driven away. The police are now looking for her. She will go to the gallows."

Maude was confused. "But Amelia, there's one thing I don't fully understand about all of this. What were you doing at a labor protest when you've never done a day's work in your life?"

The blue spong hovered over Amelia's head and throbbed and throbbed and a-throbbed, then exploded with light.

OVERNIGHT, THE NUBS on the back of Edward's shadow grew into wings. His shadow was now the shadow of a hawk, a feathered predator, magnificent and graceful, the wings fully formed, the talons sharp, the beak hooked. Soon Edward would soar across America, over prairies, mountains, canyons, cornfields, lakes and forests. He would escape mediocrity, never looking back as he fled from the horrors of conventional wisdom and mind-numbing normality.

Celie, Caitlin, and the Baum twins were at the kitchen table, helping themselves to oatmeal and warm toasted English muffins. Chan Yan-tak, Yi Yin, and Lin Kwang huddled in the far corner cleaning their revolvers, and Jenny and Edward were in the pantry discussing Maude and Minnie Fish-Griffin's new vaudeville act.

"Maude makes a fine gentlemen." Edward cut a slice of Bianka's delicious pandoro bread.

"Very dapper. The mustache is perfect." Jenny imagined herself wearing a mustache. She lifted a finger to her upper lip and marveled at the sensation. "I think I would also make a fine gentlemen."

Edward laughed. "Yes, you would, and I would make a fine lady."

Bianka fussed over the stove. She was angry with Betsy Carswell, another charlatan dispatched into the afterlife. Carswell claimed she could contact Bianka's parents, drowned on the RMS *Lusitania*, torpedoed by a German U-boat in the war. Sadly, as with David Podmore, Carswell channeled her mother, a native of Pietrapertosa in Italy, and she spoke in English. A language she never mastered. The cleaning lady found Carswell's skeleton the following morning. Detectives at the Chicago Police Department were baffled. The son of Jack the Ripper was one theory, or the grandson, or a cousin. Nobody suspected Jackie the Ripper. While Bianka fumed and peeled potatoes, the blue spong hovered over her head throb, throb, a-throbbing, while the two nubs on the back of her hawk shadow grew larger. Scratchy feathers.

"Did you ever find out who came home with Amelia last night? The owner of the smelly scarf?" Celie asked Caitlin.

"It was a friend of Amelia's. Oh, what does one call a woman who is a hobo? Anyway, she looked dreadful. Battered. The police are looking for her, something to do with the Chief of Police in Evanston being shot. I didn't hear all the details."

"How exciting."

Kamilla brushed crumbs from her dress. "We were hoping the mystery woman was Clotilda. Although, it's not like Clotilda to own a smelly scarf."

"She wasn't the smelly scarf type." Katharina brushed crumbs from her dress, the same crumbs that Kamilla had brushed from her dress that had landed on Katharina's dress. Most of Katharina's crumbs flew back onto Kamilla's dress.

Caitlin watched the airborne crumbs flying from one Baum sister to the next, then back again. "I'd forgotten all about Clotilda. Is there any news?"

Kamilla brushed the crumbs away again. "No, she vanished into thin air. The police have given up on looking for her. They think she just upped and left town, and that we imagined what we saw in the church."

Caitlin agreed with the police. It was absurd. People don't just disappear. Caitlin picked up a muffin and saw the face of Jesus Christ in it. Jesus had blueberry eyes. God came to mind. With all the goings-on at Palourde Parlor Caitlin had forgotten all about God. He was once her friend, her guiding light in the darkness. Now, without the tight corset of Catholicism cramping her passions, she was free. A godless pagan, she danced naked in the wild woods, her pendulous breasts and fat ass her offerings to the pagan world. She felt no shame or guilt. She fellated Chinamen with impunity. Now alive, she felt pain and pleasure for the first time. She fled mediocrity at the speed of light.

Celie squealed and cupped her hand to her mouth. "Oh, Edward, I've just noticed you've shaved off your mustache. Whatever for?"

"I shaved it off in preparation for…" Edward stopped. "I've got something to tell you all. I tell you this with great sorrow and also great joy. I will be leaving Palourde Parlor and starting a new job."

Caitlin looked shocked. "Where on Earth could you be going? Are you still going to be a chauffeur?"

"No, my days as a chauffeur are over. I'm starting a new life. I'm moving to Hollywood." He stood up straighter, as if the miles of highway wrapped around his spine. "I'm going to be a motion-picture star."

"An actor? You'll have to remember to hold more than a door open. Entire scripts!"

Edward laughed. "On one of Miss Maude's painting outings to Oak Street Beach, I met a film producer. One Max Dorsey. He invited me for a screen test. Apparently the camera loves me."

Caitlin suspected that it wasn't a camera that was smitten. "How exciting. You might meet Charlie Chaplin."

"Or Rudolph Valentino." Bianka held a spatula over her heart. "I saw him in *Blood and Sand*, where he played a matador. If you meet Rudolph Valentino you must tell him where I live. I need an Italian husband who is handsome. Tell him I can cook."

"I prefer John Gilbert in *Arabian Love*." Celie clutched her bosom as if a swoon was imminent. "Edward, when are you leaving?"

"I'm being picked up in an hour."

"Have you told the Clams? You'll need to tell them. They'll want to know."

He bit his lower lip. A new gesture, one he might have used for Dorsey to convey a troubled heart. "Dear me. It's all happened so suddenly. I haven't had time. I've barely had time to pack. Max is sending a car to pick me up."

"The chauffeur now has a chauffeur?"

The blue spong hovered over Edward's head, throb, throb, a-throbbing, brighter than usual. The air thickened like treacle. The pots and pans in the kitchen rattled with the same resonance as the Tibetan brass bells on the roof of the Jokhang Temple in Lhasa. The lights flickered. Edward's eyes glazed over and his body stiffened. The blue spong pushed against his chest, until the glowing orb entered his shuddering body. Edward levitated two feet off the ground, his legs dangling in the air like a marionette in the wicked Théâtre du Grand-Guignol. Kamilla screamed. Katharina fainted. The others watched in horror. Suddenly all was quiet again, as the blue spong eased itself out of Edward's chest and hovered in the corner of the kitchen as if nothing had happened. Except, it had.

Caitlin released her grip on the tabletop. "What just happened?"

Lin Kwang squeezed her hand. "Edward's shadow has received its wings from the blue spong. He now has the heart of a hawk. He can fly out of the nest and begin his epic journey away from a life of mediocrity."

"What does that mean? Who is to say what a ordinary life is and what it isn't? What may be mediocre for one person may not be run of the mill for someone else."

"A mediocre life is one where over the horizon lies a sleeping dragon that doesn't exist. You know he doesn't exist and yet you still fear him. A mediocre life is where, every minute of every day, you miss the toilet and pass water on your dreams. Life should be a blissful chaos, filled with an unpredictable wonderment of never knowing what will happen next. A life where the doors are left unlocked and strangers wander in, sit down at the table and tell you stories of other places, other times, and other worlds. Life should be a place where the branches on the question mark tree are always hanging heavy with fruit."

Caitlin understood. "After Edward leaves we'll never see him again, will we?"

"No, when you're running away from something, you should never look back."

"Like Lot's wife," Caitlin muttered under her breath. "Just like Lot's wife."

Edward regained his composure, then laughed as his shadow opened its wings and flew around the kitchen walls. He looked forward to being on screens throughout the world, inspiring and being desired by countless people. Oh, the many hearts he'd break.

Bianka tried to swat the spong with a spatula. "Go away, go away."

The three Chinamen laughed.

Kamilla answered a knock at the door.

"I'm here to pick up a Mr. Henderson." The driver, a portly man with rolled-up shirtsleeves, sweated in a tweed vest. He doffed his cloth cap. "I might be a little early."

Lin Kwang helped Edward with his bags. Caitlin, Celie, Bianka, Jenny and the Baum twins waved Edward off. A strange silence fell over the residents of Palourde Parlor as each of them felt the wing-buds and scratchy feathers growing on their shadows.

The exhausted blue spong took refuge in Amelia's bedroom.

MISSION NO 1 COMPLETE.

TWELVE

THAT AFTERNOON CHARLOTTE and Chin Wing led a funeral procession through the streets of Chinatown. Before it began, Chin Wing and Charlotte met with the families of the three young men who were gunned down by the On Leong gang: two brothers, fifteen-year-old Nan Weidong and sixteen-year-old Nan Weiping, and eighteen-year-old Zhang Kai. In the funeral home the family members circled the coffin telling stories of the deceased.

"Coins and jewelry are placed in their mouths," Chin Wing explained to Charlotte. "Then their legs are tied together so the body doesn't move if it becomes possessed by evil spirits. At a special moment chosen by the feng-shui master, the wife, mother, or some other family member, wipes the eyes of the deceased with cotton floss, then cakes are placed inside the coffin to distract the vicious dogs that wait for the dead in the Underworld."

Outside the funeral parlor, the bedding of the three young men was set alight, and when reduced to embers the procession set off through the streets of Chinatown. Chin Wing and Charlotte wore long robes of unbleached white muslin, their heads covered with hoods. The route was lined with lanterns. The coffins were in three hearses decorated with dragons, and the musicians, monks, and mourners walked behind, some carrying images of Taoist saints. Two men tossed firecrackers to scare away harmful ghosts.

After the burials, Lin Kwang drove Chin Wing and Charlotte through the bustling streets of Chinatown. Charlotte daydreamed about her fortuitous meeting with Mr. Dobson, the proprietor of Kaempfer's bird store. How she and her sisters were returning home from Holy Name Cathedral. How Mr. Dobson approached her in the street and told her about the blue spong. How, in searching for the origin of the spong, she found Wong Sing Fook in Chinatown. How she met and fell in love with gang leader Chin Wing. How long ago it seemed. Charlotte leaned out the window and inhaled the smell of roast duck and shark fin soup. This was her home now. These were her smells. This was where she belonged. Her thoughts crackled like brushfire. The timid Charlotte tending her rooftop plants was now a distant memory, a ghost. She imagined telling her parents she smoked opium and was a gangster's moll. She tried to care about their reaction, but she didn't. She tried harder. The truth was she didn't care at all.

The car pulled up outside the laundry. Wong Sing Fook was waiting for her. He was wearing a lime-green cotton hanfu, a pair of dragon slippers, and the three-inch nail on the small finger of his right hand was painted red like the bloody talon of a hawk. The two embraced. Wong Sing Fook led Charlotte through the steamy laundry and into the opium den in the rear. They lay next to each other on adjacent cots and relaxed.

"This will be the last time you come here for these dreams." Wong Sing Fook spoke quietly. "Opium is a dangerous adventure. You came here to discover the origins of the blue spong. This last dream will tell you everything you need to know."

As before, the old man appeared with two pipes, one he handed to Charlotte, the other to Wong Sing Fook. Charlotte inhaled deeply and fell back onto the couch. She closed her eyes and fell into a deep well lined with pink wool that smelled of marmalade and ginger. She examined her hands as she was falling. Her palms were saucers, her fingers forks, and then spoons. Her hair tumbled over her shoulders and grew to her feet. She fell through several worlds, one a sea of lime-green slime, another a forest of fir trees on a bed of pine cones. Charlotte landed on a garden wall covered in sweet-smelling honeysuckle. Nearby a white tigress yawned, stretched out on the grass and flexed her claws as three cubs played at her feet. One yelped when the tumbling got too rough. A translucent veil of falling orange blossoms lifted and out of the haze appeared the Emperor Kublai Khan and his three children, Dorji, Zhenjin, and Manggala. Charlotte joined the family sitting on the grass. She and the children listened as Kublai Khan told heroic tales of the hawks in the Toluid Civil War. How they fought alongside the troops. He told of how the blue spong traveled through time and space and used magnets and magic to entice people away from their mediocre lives.

"The spong is the great liberator. It liberates you from the twin hells of tedium and monotony. The spong doesn't make you a better or a worse person. It ends your mediocre life but what happens next is up to you. After leaving a mediocre life you can go anywhere, become a saint or a monster, or both. It doesn't matter. It only matters that you leave mediocrity behind." Kublai Khan threw a pack of tarot cards into the air where they dissolved, except for the Judgment card that fell at Charlotte's feet. "The Judgment card means that answering the call of the spong leads you toward an ending and then a new beginning. Charlotte, has your life changed since you met the spong?"

"It has. I've fallen in love."

"What better way to escape mediocrity than to fall in love. You will soon leave the nest. But yours is not the only eyass at the Palourde Parlor nest. There are nine other hawks that will flee that nest before the spong returns home to me. One has already flown. Do you have any questions?"

"Yes, why me? Why did the spong choose me? Why did the spong come to Palourde Parlor?"

"A very good question. I sent out an angel to find people who lead mediocre lives. You and your sisters were chosen, as you were leading lives of complete and utter tedium bordering on catatonic. Your house is a vortex of mediocrity. You may recognize my angel."

A woman wearing a red and gold diaphanous gown walked out of the trunk of a nearby tree. Her head shaved, a halo of blue flames burned around her pate. She was barefoot and carried in her arms a Siamese cat with blue almond-shaped eyes. The cat struggled, hissed and spat at Charlotte.

"Clotilda? Is that you?" At the sound of Charlotte's voice, Clotilda faded away. "Clotilda is an angel?"

"Yes, I sent her out into the world and she found you and your two sisters in the deathly grip of mediocrity." Kublai Khan climbed to his feet and whistled. A falcon flew down from a nearby tree, landing on his forearm. Kublai Khan opened the door in the hawk's chest and out flew the blue spong, throb, throb, a-throbbing, then exploding and sending out of light. The spong attached itself to Charlotte's chest, pressing into her, until it entered her body. Charlotte gasped as she floated into the air like a tethered balloon. Moments later the spong left her body.

MISSION NO 2 COMPLETE.

As Charlotte lay on the grass unconscious, two pandas ambled past chewing bamboo shoots. A rainbow appeared and Charlotte tumbled back into the pink well that smelled of marmalade and ginger. She woke in the arms of Chin Wing. "Charlotte, do not be alarmed, but while you were dreaming, something has occurred. I have to leave for San Francisco. I am in danger and also my family."

"When are you leaving?"

"Now. I have to leave right now."

"I'm coming with you." Charlotte gripped his hand. "We must stop off at the house to tell my sisters."

"We don't have time."

Lin Kwang carried Charlotte to the car. He climbed into the driver's seat and drove the couple out of Chinatown.

"Take us to Dearborn Street Station." Chin Wing pulled down the window blinds. "We will board the Pacific Limited that will take us to San Francisco. Chan Yan-tak and Yi-Yin will travel with us. They're waiting for us at the station. After you drop us off, you will visit Charlotte's sisters and tell them what's happened. Then you must follow me to San Francisco on the next train."

Still drowsy from the opium, Charlotte heard gunfire, the ra-ta-tat of a Thompson submachine gun. A bullet shattered the windshield, missing Lin Kwang by inches. Another tore into the trunk. Chin Wing fired his revolver out the window as Lin Kwang drove faster, skidded around a corner and headed for Dearborn Street Station. The gunfire stopped. Charlotte fell into Chin Wing's arms. "I'll never come back here." The wings on her shadow stretched out and shimmered in the waning light. Charlotte felt tingling in her spine as she shed the skin of mediocrity. It lay at her feet, an ugly festering mess. She opened the door and kicked it out into the street.

After dropping the couple off, Lin Kwang drove north to Chestnut Street, to Palourde Parlor, where he found Maude and Amelia in the drawing room with Lizzie Ball. Lin Kwang explained how the On Leong had taken control of Chinatown, how Chin Wing's life was in danger, and how he and Charlotte had left for San Francisco.

Amelia listened. "Did she say when she was returning?"

"No." Lin Kwang said nothing more. He knew Charlotte would never return. Once the flight from mediocrity began there was no turning back.

The Clam sisters had never been parted. As children they were inseparable; when one sister left the room the other two felt abandoned, became anxious. They fretted until the absent sister returned. Even now, one sister, on greeting another, asked where the third was. "Where's Amelia?" Charlotte asked Maude. "Where's Maude?" Charlotte asked Amelia. "Where's Charlotte," Maude asked Amelia, and so on. Now Charlotte had eloped to San Francisco with a Chinese triad gang leader. Both Maude and Amelia tried to care about Charlotte's sudden departure. In truth, neither did. They were too wrapped up in their own flights from mediocrity. Maude's future was male impersonation on the vaudeville stage and Amelia's to end the tyranny of the ruling class.

The blue spong hovered in the stairwell, throbbing with pride.

LIN KWANG VISITED Caitlin downstairs. "Come with me to San Francisco. I love you."

"I love you too, but I have other plans." Lin Kwang saw Caitlin's hawk shadow fly across her bedroom wall. He knew that nothing could stop Caitlin's flight from mediocrity. "I may open a tea shop in Vermont." Caitlin shrugged her shoulders. "Or I may go to Paris and study painting at the Académie Julian, or I may go back to Ireland and write children's books. I don't know. But I'm leaving today for New York, to Greenwich Village, and after that I don't know where I'm going."

"But you'll need money," said Lin Kwang.

"I've been putting money into a Rainy Day Fund."

Caitlin's earnings from fellating Hip Sing bodyguards added up to $200. However, her savings were augmented by the illicit sale of books from Richard Clam's library. She smuggled Robert Carpenter, a disreputable rare book dealer, into Palourde Parlor. She'd met Carpenter at Brentano's Bookstore when they were reaching for the same copy of Charles Dickens' *Oliver Twist*. After striking up a conversation, followed by tea and a honey bun, they concocted a mutually beneficial plan. Caitlin snuck the shifty Carpenter into Palourde Parlor, where he compiled a list of books he was interested in purchasing. Caitlin then smuggled the tomes out of the house in a carpetbag, delivering them to Carpenter on a park bench overlooking Oak Street Beach and Lake Michigan. She was paid $25,000 in cash, which she placed in the Lake Shore Trust and Savings Bank. The books included a first edition of Miguel de Cervantes' *Don Quixote*, dated 1605, and one copy each of Ptolemy's *Geographia Cosmographia*, and Nicolaus Copernicus' *On the Revolutions of the Heavenly Spheres*. Nobody noticed the books were missing. Nobody noticed the books were there.

Earlier that morning the blue spong had entered Caitlin's chest. At the time, she was reclining in a bathtub of soapy water, dwelling on the past. She recalled her impoverished childhood, growing up in Mainistir Ó dTorna, a village near the windswept coast of County Kerry in Ireland. Running barefoot through the gravestones at the ruins of Abbeydorney, where ghosts of Cistercian monks haunted the walls and hallways. How, with her parents, at the age of ten, she boarded the SS *Teutonic* in Queenstown, crossing the Atlantic to New York in 1900. The long train journey from New York to Chicago, where her parents worked in a meatpacking plant on the South Side. Her parents had died within months of each other, leaving Caitlin orphaned. At sixteen she answered an advertisement in the *Chicago Tribune* and was hired at Palourde Parlor. Caitlin had packed her luggage, including pilfered copies of William Blake's *The Book of Urizen* and a Gutenberg Bible she was saving for an emergency.

"At least let me drive you to the station." Lin Kwang held her hand.

"I'd like that." Caitlin kissed him on the lips, then unbuttoned his trousers and fellated him one last time. He handed her a ten dollar bill. She took it.

At Dearborn Street station Kwang parked the car and gave the hand crank to a hobo. "Take the car, it's yours." Then he boarded the train to San Francisco, while Caitlin caught the train to New York. As the train pulled out of the station, Caitlin felt the hawk's heart beating in her chest, and the scratchy wings on her shadow.

MISSION NO 3 COMPLETE.

If the blue spong could speak (which it couldn't) it would have giggled like a schoolgirl. If it could dance (which it couldn't do either), it would have danced a merry Irish jig.

Caitlin's departure went unnoticed until Amelia summoned the Irish housekeeper to the drawing room and the bell went unanswered. Nobody seemed surprised or upset by Caitlin's exodus or, indeed, affected by it in any way. While the walls of Palourde Parlor remained sturdy and strong, the foundations of tradition, ethics and moral values, crumbled beneath the occupants' feet. The interior fixtures and fittings were in peril, with religion hanging by a thread, the hierarchical social pyramid twisted and rotten on the floor, and the vice-like grip of mediocrity an ever-growing puddle of slime on the floor. As the spong's nestlings took flight, each deflated more air out of this hellish windbag balloon of normality.

"Caitlin's room is empty. I think she left this morning with Lin Kwang." Bianka wasn't surprised.

"Perhaps they've eloped." Celie laughed, oblivious to how close to the truth she was. "Perhaps he has taken her to China to meet his family."

The two women laughed.

That morning Celie saw her hawk shadow fly across her bedroom wall. She was neither startled by it, nor did she wonder what it was. Amelia and Maude too had seen their hawk shadows that morning. After Caitlin's departure, the spong focused on the Baum twins, throb, throb, a-throbbing. Since moving into Palourde Parlor, the Baum twins had fallen under the spell of the blue spong. Now, free from the teachings of Martin Luther, Kamilla was invigorated, Katharina giddy with fanciful notions. The nubs on the hawk shadows of the Baum twins now had scratchy feathers. It was time to fly.

That afternoon the twins ventured out through the tall wrought-iron curlicue gates at Palourde Parlor. From birth, the Baum twins dressed identically. Sometimes their parents couldn't tell them apart, other times they couldn't tell themselves apart and, more than once, one or other of the Baum twins glanced into the mirror and saw her sister looking back at her. Today they wore a blue silk georgette crepe dress with a lace collar, flared skirt, a cloche hat, and tan suede shoes with a silk bow. They headed downtown to the affluent stores hidden in canyons of skyscrapers. They stopped outside Roberts & Co., diamond importers, at 36 S. State Street, and peered in the window. Kamilla entered, browsed for a while, then asked to see a wedding ring from the display case. When the sales assistant, a tall skeletal man with cracking knuckles, handed her the ring, she promptly fainted. The staff gathered around her. One young woman waved smelling salts under her nose while another fanned her with a receipt. Meanwhile, Katharina entered the store and pocketed a gold and sapphire necklace and a Black, Starr & Frost string of pearls. Slipping them into her purse, she walked out of the store. The two sisters met later at the Sally Frost Tearooms over tea and chocolate éclairs.

"I never realized stealing was so easy." Katharina poured black tea into Kamilla's cup. "These chocolate éclairs are delicious. Do you think they would give us the recipe?"

"Most likely not. Stealing is really just a conjuring trick, sleight of hand. I was amused that you were seen stealing the jewelry but a witness gave the description of a woman in a blue silk dress and then pointed at me and said, 'That's her. She's the thief.' Of course, I couldn't have stolen the jewelry because I was on the floor being revived. Much confusion ensued."

"I had already made my getaway." Katharina laughed.

The Baum twins' pilfering had nothing to do with material gain. Their interest in stealing was purely sexual. When Katharina slipped the jewelry into her purse at Roberts & Co. she experienced an explosive orgasm, as did Kamilla when she fainted. At Sally Frost's Tearooms both twins were moist between their legs as they sipped lapsang souchong. On their way home they stopped off at Barnett & Co. to pull the same ruse, netting a white-gold pendant with a diamond halo and a pair of Art Deco gold cufflinks. In Bughouse Square they sat on a bench recovering from the shuddering orgasms. They were entirely unprepared for this blossoming of their sexuality. The Rev. Eric Gustavson at Holy Trinity Church had failed to mention orgasms in his sermons. While barking out his commentary on this, that, and the other, the handsome Scandinavian waxed lyrical about being "Transformed in the Image of God" and "Bathing in the Blood of the Lamb," but on the subject of sexual orgasms he was silent. Jesus didn't mention them either, not even in his pièce de résistance, the Sermon on the Mount.

NO SOONER HAD the Baum twins returned to Palourde Parlor than the doorbell rang. It was two policemen. Celie answered it.

"We'd like to speak to a Miss Amelia Clam."

"Please come in. Can I tell her what it's about?"

"We need to question her about a woman we're looking for, a Miss Lizzie Ball. We believe Miss Clam has information about a murder."

Celie delivered the message to Amelia, who skipped down the staircase, across the hallway, smiling from ear to ear. Then she stopped, unclipped the silver clasp on her purse, pulled out a revolver, then fired twice, one bullet each into the skulls of the cops. They dropped to the floor like sacks of potatoes.

Bianka, Jenny and the Baum twins ran upstairs into the hallway. Antonio and Lizzie Ball rushed down from upstairs, closely followed by Maude and Minnie Fish-Griffin. They all met in the hallway, circling the dead cops. Two pools of blood poured out onto the tiled floor, growing ever bigger, until they met and formed a lake that resembled a map of Australia. The spong hovered in the stairwell, throb, throb, a-throbbing, and then exploding with blue light. The beams ricocheted off the walls, then fizzled out like spent fireworks. The air was thick with silence. Jenny held her breath, frightened to inhale in case the sound alerted more police. They would burst in, guns blazing. She would be caught in the crossfire. The Baum twins held onto each other tightly. Amelia slipped the smoking gun back into her purse. A full minute passed.

"What are we going to do now?" Maude stared at the brace of

lifeless cops, dead as bug-eyed herring on a fishmonger's slab. "How are we to dispose of them? We can't leave them here in the hallway. We must bury them in the garden. We need to clean up this blood. What a mess."

Celie suggested burying them under the rose bushes.

"Why don't we roll them up in rugs and dump them in Lake Michigan." Minnie Fish-Griffin knelt down and removed the cops' wallets. "We can't leave them here."

"They look quite peaceful." Kamilla had never seen a dead body before.

JENNY WAS MOIST between her legs. "Do you think their spirits are still in the room? They may be watching and listening to us." The blue spong hovered over her, throb, throb, throbbing, all the time draining putrid blobs of mediocrity from her life. She stared at the dead cops. The two corpses unleashed her hitherto hidden necrophiliac passions. One was a young blond, the other older, stocky, with a mass of black hair. She fought the urge to kneel in the blood, unbutton their flies, slide her hand into their underthings and massage their manhoods. She wondered if their balls were still warm and soft, or whether rigor mortis had set in. Jenny closed her eyes, imagined mounting one dead cop, then the other, Brünnhilde wearing a horned Viking helmet, riding them all the way to Valhalla. Jenny was so horny she could make a dead man come.

The pool of blood grew larger and the circle of assembled residents of Palourde Parlor took two steps back. Lizzie Ball buried her face in her hands. "They're going to think I killed these two cops as well as the chief of the Evanston police department. That's three dead cops now."

"I'll dispose of the bodies. I know what to do." Bianka stepped forward. "Just leave it to me. I want you all to remain as still and silent as possible. Don't be frightened by what you are about to see."

Bianka flexed her fingers like a virtuoso pianist about to play Franz Liszt's *Rêves et fantasies* in a concert hall. She chanted quietly:

"Dies irae, dies illa.
Solvet Saeclum in favilla
Teste Satan cum sibylla.
Quantos tremor est futurus
Quando Vindex est venturus
Cuncta stricte discussurus.
Dies irae, dies illa!"

Jenny shivered as a damp chill fell over the hallway. On the hall stand a potted aspidistra withered and died, the crisp leaves fell to the ground like confetti at a corpse wedding. Walking sticks in a tall ceramic pot were dusted with a thin layer of frost and hats froze on the hat stand. Antonio slid his arms around Amelia's waist and pulled her tightly into him. He felt the warm breath of Baphomet, the Sabbatic goat, on his face. He could smell its sourness, like rotting vegetables. Maude and Minnie hid behind a pillar, clinging to each other, their eyes closed, their hearts pumping. The Baum twins held hands and stood firm like oak trees. Bianka's eyes lit up into fiery red flames as she breathed heavily, panting. She threw back her head and wailed, a wail dragged up kicking and screaming from the bowels of hell. Cracks appeared in the floor and a river of mercury snaked across the hallway, splitting into rivulets, then into babbling brooks. A rotting giraffe's head pushed through the ceiling and tiny flecks of wallpaper began to tear away from the walls. A wind whipped up the paper blizzard like a snowstorm, then the paper flecks descended on the two cops like piranha fish. In the feeding frenzy, the room jerked slightly to the right, clicking like clockwork. The flecks of wallpaper soaked up the blood and returned to the wall. Then, as suddenly as it began, the hallway returned to normal, except for the two bleached-white skeletons on the floor.

BIANKA STOOD FIRM. "Don't touch the wallpaper. It bleeds to the touch."

If anyone connected Bianka's invocation of Beelzebub to the recent murders of clairvoyants, they said nothing. Not one word. Mediocrity was losing its grip on the spong's remaining hatchlings at Palourde Parlor. Mediocrity clung to the cliff top of their consciousness while the blue spong mercilessly stomped on its fingers. After burying the cops' skeletons under the roses, Antonio returned to the drawing room. He paced the floor. "We need to leave now. They are going to come looking for those cops. We must get to New York. Then leave the country. Russia…we must get to Russia. Amelia, I will return in one hour with a car. I must find Dariusz. He can help us."

It was twilight outside, still warm. A cool breeze blew in off Lake Michigan as couplings of sweethearts paraded arm-in-arm through the streets. In the distance Antonio heard the haunting sound of hungry seagulls screeching as he headed for the Green Mask Café.

After Antonio left, Amelia ran upstairs and hastily packed a bag. The blue spong followed her and hovered near the ceiling cornice, throb, throb, a-throbbing, occasionally sending out light. Reaching for her hat, Amelia caught a glimpse of her reflection in the mirror. No longer was she the shy young woman whose only sin was a secret passion for sweetmeats, pastries, and dainties from Eckert's Bakery. She was now a disheveled and committed revolutionary, a three-time cop killer. The spong fell upon her chest and pushed inside. She felt its fluttering heartbeat. Amelia's body shook, levitated two feet above the ground and then dropped to the floor like a rag doll. Now, with the hawk's heart beating in her chest, Amelia began her rapid flight from mediocrity. She would seek exile in Russia, follow in the footsteps of Emma Goldman and crush the ruling class. She would join the glorious revolution. As Amelia descended the stairs she was followed by her hawk shadow, wings outstretched, flying and swooping across the staircase wall. Lizzie was waiting for her.

"Are you ready to leave your privileged life?"

"What life? This is no life. Now tell me, who is this Dariusz?"

"A Polish friend, a fellow anarchist. He escaped Poland and came to Chicago after being accused of plotting to kill the Polish Prime Minister, Jan Kanty Steczkowski. The Polish authorities are still looking for him."

"And he can help us escape?"

"He'll know what to do."

Fifty minutes later Antonio returned. "Come on, let's go, there's a car waiting in the alley." Amelia and Lizzie climbed into the back of a Model-T Ford truck with *Pioneer Tea Company* printed on the side. "Szybko wskakuj do samochodu! Musimy natychmiast jechać do Nowego Jorku, a stamtąd do Rosji," said Dariusz, a raggedly dressed bearded man with a cigarette dangling from his lips. Dariusz squinted from a coil of smoke spiraling up into his eye. The truck headed south out of Chicago, then followed Lake Michigan into Indiana, then east toward the Atlantic Ocean. At Palourde Parlor the smell of chaos filled the air and the blue spong hid under Amelia's bed. It was exhausted.

MISSION NO 4 COMPLETE.

THIRTEEN

The following morning Celestynka "Celie" Majewski sat alone in her room, relaxing in an armchair, eyes closed, her head resting on a fussy antimacassar. The blue spong had entered her body during the night, while she slept. She could feel its hawkish heartbeat and scratchy feathers on the wings of her shadow. Celie, daughter of Polish immigrants, Radosław and Rozyczka Majewski, was born in Chicago on a cold winter night in a blizzard that produced snowdrifts ten feet high. Her father was a drunk, her mother a troubled soul given to violent fits and tantrums. The reason they left Poland was unclear, never spoken of. But whatever it was, they were damaged by it. Celie was estranged from them. Her parents had no idea where she was. They never strayed from the Polish ghetto on Milwaukee Avenue, so their paths never crossed. Celie's suitcase lay on the bed, packed and ready. It contained her most treasured possessions, a copy of *Opowiesc Wigilijna* by Charles Dickens, a necklace that belonged to her grandmother, and a ring given to her by her sweetheart, lost in the Great War in Europe. She removed the newspaper cuttings of Harry Houdini from the walls of her room. Houdini was her childhood hero. He could be tied up in chains, hung on a rope, dropped into a river, and then miraculously escape. Escape from bondage. Now it was her turn to escape. Escape a mediocre life, a life of drudgery, cleaning, dusting, housemaid's knee. Her new job at Miss Sadie's Galloping Stallion Riding Stables for Gentlemen with Equestrian Taste excited her. She opened her suitcase, took out a riding crop and whipped the pillow. The pillow smarted. She could feel the pillow's pain. The pillow's pain excited her. "I can see that I'm going to have to break you in before I saddle you up and mount you," Celie sneered at the pillow. "You're a very naughty pillow." She thwacked the pillow again and again and again, until it submitted to her will, giving itself over to pleasure and pain. Celie mounted the sack of feathers and rode it around the room, striking it repeatedly with the riding crop until it burst, sending feathers into the air. Celie shook out the remaining feathers and danced in the blizzard of plumage. She wore her best outfit, a beaded embroidered silk chiffon dress with a matching coat, a draped crown hat of visca straw cloth with clusters of fruit, and a pair of calfskin shoes. Celie quietly left the house by the front door. As she closed the gate, she sighed, straightened her hat, then set off down the street picking feathers off her clothes and smiling. She never looked back.

The spong hovered in the hallway, throb, throb, a-throbbing, like a miniature blue sun.

MISSION NO 5 COMPLETE.

AFTER BREAKFAST BIANKA washed dishes in the sink, while Jenny dried them. They spoke quietly of family and days gone by. The Baum twins, in the staff dining room, read an article on the front page of the *Chicago Tribune*. The headline read: "Daring Jewel Thieves Strike Twice. Police See Double." The Baums' heists at Roberts & Co. and Barnett & Co. made the front page. The police suspected a pair of twins. Katharina and Kamilla moistened and shuddered as waves of pleasure radiated through their bodies. Katharina whimpered like a kitten lost in the woods, but Kamilla's orgasm was explosive. She cried out in rasping gasps and stifled screams, followed by a lengthy banshee wail. Even the blue spong took cover behind the drapes.

"What was that?" Bianka stood in the doorway clutching a wet spatula. "It sounded like Sir Arthur Conan Doyle's hound of the Baskervilles."

"It was nothing." Katharina covered for her sister. "Kamilla was practicing her lion's roar."

"Lion's roar?"

"Yes, her lion's roar. Kamilla is practicing animal noises."

"Oh!"

"The WMAZ radio station is having a competition for people who impersonate animals. Kamilla is thinking of entering."

"Oh!" Bianka shrugged her shoulders.

An awkward silence fell over the room.

"Did you know that Celie has left us?" Jenny walked into the dining room. "This morning, early before anyone was awake. Maude and Minnie are also gone. They're auditioning this afternoon with the Barnaby Bixby Traveling Vaudeville Circus. They're calling their act Mack and Mabel, Mack being Maude, of course, who makes a very convincing man if you ask me. I thought I detected stubble on her chin this morning. And she's taken to smoking a cigar, says it makes her voice deeper."

Bianka changed the subject. "So, the WMAZ radio station competition for people who impersonate animals. What other animal noises do you do, beside the lion?"

"The ant." Kamilla regretted the word as soon as it left her lips.

"The ant! What kind of noise does an ant make?"

Kamilla was saved by three rapid knocks at the basement door. The women froze. Jenny hoped it wasn't the police looking for Amelia. Bianka hoped it wasn't the police looking for her. The Baum twins hoped it wasn't the police looking for them. Katharina and Kamilla opened their identical purses and pulled out the Colt Police Positive Specials they'd lifted from the two cops now fertilizing the roses in the garden. Kamilla crouched behind the Gainaday electric washing machine and Katharina hid in the larder. Jenny answered the door and stepped outside, pulling the door shut behind her. The women inside heard a brief exchange. Jenny returned with an envelope. "It's a letter for you." She handed an envelope to Bianka, who opened it, quietly read the single sheet of paper, then folded it and slipped it into the pocket of her apron.

"It's nothing important."

THE LETTER WAS from Ronald Ginstrap, a lawyer with Ginstrap, Ginstrap and Lovell, requesting Miss Bianka Morietta visit his office at her earliest convenience to hear something to her advantage. The spong hovered over the sink, throb, throb, a-throbbing, and gleaming.

LATER THAT DAY Bianka caught the elevated train to Ravenswood to visit a Miss Jessica Swanthorpe, a spiritualist she had found through an ad in the *Chicago American* claiming she could contact the dead through Bright Moon, an Indian spirit guide. Bianka turned onto leafy Eastwood Avenue with its neat gardens and manicured lawns and hedges. It was a gloriously sunny day with nervous squirrels darting up trees and rabbits hopping between the rows of two-flat dwellings. Bianka reached 2224, climbed up the porch steps, lifted the knocker and brought it down three times.

A tall woman in her early fifties answered. "May I help you?"

"I'm Bianka Morietta, I called and made an appointment earlier.

I'm a little early."

"Come in. I apologize for being reticent on the phone. There has been a spate of clairvoyants being horribly murdered by a maniac. They say it might be the son of Jack the Ripper."

"Oh, yes, I've been reading about it in the newspaper."

"I'm only seeing women for now. It's safer." Swanthorpe led Bianka into a small cluttered parlor. "You can't be too careful. Now, you said you want to contact your parents who died on the *Lusitania*." Swanthorpe drooped then. "How terribly tragic. I have spoken to many of the dead from that passenger ship through Bright Moon, and also the *Titanic*. Please sit here at the table."

Fifteen minutes later, Jessica Swanthorpe was a bleached white skeleton and the wallpaper in her parlor bled to the touch. Swanthorpe failed to live up to her promise as advertised in the *Chicago American*. She couldn't speak to the dead, with or without Bright Moon, her Indian spirit guide. She was a fraud. Bianka was disappointed and the diminutive Italian cook didn't take disappointment well. After pocketing jewelry and a small amount of cash, Bianka caught the train downtown. Outside the Madison Avenue offices of Ginstrap, Ginstrap and Lovell, Bianka checked the address on the envelope, took a deep breath and entered. She introduced herself to the receptionist, a mousy girl, about seventeen years of age with thick spectacles and a lopsided mouth she tried to rectify with lipstick. She failed. She looked like a circus clown. The girl steered Bianka into the office of Gordon Ginstrap, a balding man in his late forties wearing a smart suit and expensive shoes.

"I'll get straight to the point. Your late aunt, Isabella Martinelli..." He read the Last Will and Testament of Bianka's estranged aunt. Bianka stopped listening. Her aunt owned several trattorias in Chicago and had taken her in after the death of her parents, and the subsequent death of her aunt in New York. Martinelli taught Bianka how to cook but, after an argument over a recipe for *pasta con le sarde* turned violent, Bianka struck out on her own, ending up in the bubble of mediocrity that was Palourde Parlor. After signing forms, Bianka accepted a check from Gordon Ginstrap, folded it and slid it into her purse. It wasn't until she deposited the check into her bank that she saw it was for $300,000. She was light-headed. Outside the bank she darted down an alley and sank into an armchair next to the trash. The blue spong hovered above her head, throb, throb, a-throbbing, sending out beams of steel-blue light. Then it descended, pushed into her chest, until a hawk's heart beat inside of her. The magnetic pull of the spong left her longing to cook real Italian food again, *lasagne verdi al forno* instead of pan-roasted duck breast, *fettuccine al burro* instead of meatloaf and a sad medley of vegetables. She brushed herself off and hailed a cab that took her to the Lexington Hotel, where she booked a suite under the name Florentina Donati.

MISSION NO 6 COMPLETE.

THE TERRIBLE DEATH of clairvoyant Jessica Swanthorpe was followed by the demise of three other Chicago mediums, all killed and left as bleached-white skeletons in musty drawing rooms with bleeding wallpaper. Then as suddenly as they began, the murders stopped. Six months later they started up again in Canada.

FOURTEEN

ARM IN ARM, Maude and Minnie turned into the litter-strewn alley behind Hooley's Theater. They entered the stage door to this 1,500-seat concert hall where Barnaby Bixby's Traveling Vaudeville Circus auditioned new acts. Hooley's was a decrepit playhouse built in 1872, a relic of productions like *The Prisoner of Zenda* and *Gay Parisiennes*, along with minstrel shows and operettas like Jacques Offenbach's *La belle Hélène.* There was a rumor Hooley's was closing down. Barnaby Bixby's Traveling Vaudeville Circus, a nomadic variety show, toured the world nine months of the year. Backstage, Maude and Minnie joined a line of singers, dancers, acrobats, banjo players, hypnotists, ventriloquists, an act with poodles and another with a sea lion. The women had taken a cab from Palourde Parlor to the theater, asking to be dropped off at the end of the street, not wishing to appear affluent. They were struggling actors.

Minnie giggled. "Do you think that cab driver knew you were a girl?"

"He called me sir, so I'm guessing no."

"Pity. We want people to think you're a girl dressed as a man. If they think you're a man dressed up as a man, it undermines our intentions."

"I hadn't thought of that."

Maude changed into her costume. The duo waited an hour. Only one act left to go. Onstage, Elsie the Ozark Nightingale, a mess of red hair piled atop her head, warbled through "She's only a bird in a gilded cage, a beautiful sight to see. You may think she's happy and free from care, she's not, though she seems to be." The song reminded Maude of her own gilded cage, Palourde Parlor. She thought about Charlotte and her caged parrots, the blue spong she released and allowed to fly around the house. How it throbbed and throbbed, then exploded, illuminating Maude's reverie, which was only broken when Elsie the Ozark Nightingale was silenced by a short, sharp, British voice from the stalls: "Thank you. You were absolutely dreadful. Have you considered working in a chicken farm, a job, I believe, you are eminently suited for. Next!"

Minnie nudged Maude. "We're on." Minnie walked onto the stage, sat at an old upright piano and began to play. It was badly out of tune. Minnie grimaced.

"Don't worry about that, play the best you can." Barnaby Bixby waved his cigar, then slumped back into his seat in the eighth row.

Maude strutted onto the stage dressed as a Piccadilly Swell, dapper in a top hat, dress coat, a green carnation, spats and silver-topped walking cane. Backstage, the sea lion honked loudly, and a stagehand hammered on the catwalk above her head. Maude sang "Burlington Bertie." "I'm Bert, p'raps you've heard of me. Bert, you've had word of me, jogging along, hearty and strong, living on plates of fresh air. I dress up in fashion, and when I am feeling depressed, I shave from my cuff all the whiskers and fluff, stick my hat on and toddle up West."

Barnaby Bixby, a man in his late fifties in an ill-fitting suit and black eyebrows like torpid caterpillars, was a veritable legend in the world of vaudeville. A veteran of British freak shows, circuses and music halls, Bixby was a brilliant, arrogant and obnoxious man. He had a fondness for cocaine, enhancing his cantankerous nature. Bixby slumped in his seat, his eyes focused on the stage, pupils like pinheads. Next to him on one side was his director, Tom Spinard, on the other a sleeping bristly-faced man. Maude continued with the second verse. "I'm Burlington Bertie, I rise at ten thirty, and saunter along like a toff. I walk down the Strand with my gloves on my hand, then I walk down again with them off."

"Stop! Stop! Stop!" Bixby launched into a coughing fit. "We're leaving tomorrow, so you can rehearse on the ship."

Maude was taken aback. "What ship?"

"Tomorrow we leave by train for New York, then we embark on the *Saturnia* for London. My dears, we open at the Prince of Wales Theatre in eight weeks! You will be at Dearborn Street Station at ten a.m. and don't be late, acts like yours are a dime a dozen. Next!"

A stagehand hustled the two women off the stage. Outside in the alley, Maude and Minnie tried to contain their excitement.

"We're leaving tomorrow for Europe." Maude clapped her hands together. "It happened so fast. I'm not sure if I'm ready. Yes, I am ready. No I'm not. Yes, I am. What am I saying? I think I'm going to faint."

However, Minnie was the one who fainted.

After the robberies at Roberts & Co. and Barnett & Co., the police were in hot pursuit of a pair of female twins. It was only a matter of time before the Baums were arrested and thrown into the Brideswell Women's Correctional Center. With Jenny's help, the twins changed their appearance. Jenny dyed Kamilla's hair light brown and Katharina's black with Q-Ban hair color. They had previously been blondes. They also raided Charlotte and Amelia's closet for clothes. After an hour or so, Katharina looked like a flapper, adopting a giggly, gregarious, persona, while Kamilla was transformed into a nervous mousy librarian with round spectacles. The spong hovered over the twins, observing them, and throb, throb, a-throbbing. The spong entered their bodies during the night. Now they were eager to flee their lives of mediocrity, throw a pack of cards in the air and let them fall wherever they may. The twins planned to drive west, first stop Minneapolis, second stop unknown. Both Baum sisters could drive. Their father had taught them. He was runner-up in the 1920 Indianapolis 500, narrowly beaten by Gaston Chevrolet in a Frontenac. A daredevil, Charles Baum craved adventure. The walls of his office were covered with framed photographs of him wrestling a lion, crossing mountains in a hot air balloon, and canoeing on the Orinoco River in Venezuela. He was not in the slightest bit mediocre. However, his twin daughters were. So mediocre, in fact, it was painful for him to watch them. They were runts in his litter.

Since Edward's flight from Palourde Parlor, the Clams' Kelly green Buick convertible collected dust in the garage. A pair of robins eyed it as a possible nesting place. The Baum twins threw a suitcase onto the back seat. They hugged Jenny, then Katharina jumped into the driver's seat, Kamilla next to her. They headed north, west on Irving Park Road, then north of Milwaukee Ave. It was mid-afternoon, not much traffic. Katharina parked outside the Papanek-Kovac Bank on N. Milwaukee Ave. She kept the engine running while Kamilla adjusted her spectacles and entered the building. She was the only customer. There were three employees, two tellers and the bank manager, a Mr. Wilkinson, an elderly balding man who rode a bicycle to work. Today he was irritable because his wife forgot to pack his sandwiches for lunch. He was hungry. One teller was a bored-looking young man with acne, the other an angry woman in her mid-forties. Kamilla pulled a gun from her purse.

"You and you lie face down on the floor. You fill this bag." The two men lay on the floor, while the woman filled the bag with cash. Then Kamilla ordered her to lie on the floor. "Now count slowly to one hundred before anyone moves. Thank you for your generosity. Enjoy the rest of your day."

Kamilla slipped the gun into her purse, calmly walked out of the bank and climbed into the car. Katharina drove west into the Illinois countryside. Occasionally the car swerved as multiple orgasms shot through the Baum twins—they felt much like a sneeze of the genitals, a rising tingling, followed by a throb, throb, a-throbbing, like the blue spong. Then a gush.

"Stop the car," rasped Kamilla between orgasms.

"We can't, we have to go on, aaaarrggghhh!" As the next wave of pleasure crested, Kamilla glanced into the rear-view mirror and spied a putrid festering ball of mediocrity becoming smaller and smaller. She had bitten her lip until blood spilt before the spong faded from view.

MISSIONS NO 7 & No 8 COMPLETE.

FIFTEEN

THE FOLLOWING MORNING Maude lay in bed staring at the ceiling. When she and Minnie auditioned for Barnaby Bixby she hadn't planned on being hired on the spot. Minnie lay next to her. "We don't have much time, Maude."

"Are you sure we've packed enough clothes?"

"We can buy clothes in New York and London."

"What about costumes?"

"We can't carry more than one suitcase each. We'll go to Savile Row in London, a street of tailors, and we'll order you the best men's clothes money can buy, also a silver-topped cane and a top hat."

Minnie glowed at the prospect of performing in London. She was a free spirit. From childhood, Minnie rebelled. At eighteen months, taking her first steps, when her mother called to her, "Minnie come to Mama, come to Mama," Minnie headed in the opposite direction. Minnie was not mediocre. Sadly, Maude was. Or she used to be. The blue spong had entered Maude overnight. She was ready for her flight from mediocrity.

Dearborn Street Station was a Romanesque revival pink granite and red brick building, bustling with irritable people weighed down with luggage. Crying children were dragged like rag dolls through the crowds. Maude and Minnie bought tickets, found the platform, and joined the other acts in the Barnaby Bixby Traveling Vaudeville Circus: Mysterious Mahendra, Master of the Human Mind, Kate W. Simmons and Her Poster Pirouettes, a classical dancing carnival, Lee and his Hypnotic Performances, and Roberto the Great and His Infamous Dogs. Stepping onto the train, Maude paused. She heard a noise above the din of the crowded station. It was the death rattle of her mediocrity dying in the gutter.

MISSION NO 9 COMPLETE.

Only Jenny Susskind remained at Palourde Parlor, alone in this four-story house, empty but for its echoes, its ghosts, and its wilting mediocrity. She stood in the hallway, stared up into the stairwell and sang "Habanera" from *Carmen:*

"L'amour est un oiseau rebelle
L'amour est un oiseau rebelle
Que nul ne peut apprivoiser,
Et c'est bien en vain qu'on l'appelle,
S'il lui convient de refuser.
Rien n'y fait, menace ou prière;
L'un parle bien, l'autre se tait,
Et c'est l'autre que je préfère;
Il n'a rien dit mais il me plaît."

Jenny laughed at the absurdity of it all.

The spong hovered nearby, throb, throb, a-throbbing, and when it exploded with the most extraordinary shade of bluish light, nine hatchlings fled the mediocrity of Palourde Parlor: Edward to be a screen idol; Charlotte to wed a Hip Sing leader; Amelia to join revolutionaries in Russia; Celie to a brothel for men with equestrian taste; Caitlin to New York and beyond; Maude to be a male impersonator; Bianka to eviscerate fraudulent clairvoyants; and Katharina and Kamilla to become bank robbers on the run. The blue spong attached itself to Jenny's chest and pushed inside, until she felt the breath of hawk wings on her shadow, the scratchy feathers. Jenny wandered into the library and perused the books. Taking down a copy of *Alice Through the Looking Glass,* written by Lewis Carroll, she read the first two lines out loud: "One thing was certain, that the white kitten had had nothing to do with it: — it was the black kitten's fault entirely. For the white kitten had been having its face washed by the old cat for the last quarter of an hour (and bearing it pretty well, considering); so you see that it couldn't have had any hand in the mischief."

Jenny closed her eyes for a moment. When she opened them, a black kitten was curled up asleep in her lap. "Are you getting into mischief?" The kitten didn't answer. Not at first. Jenny read more of the book and as she read she faded from sight. By page ten Jenny Susskind vanished altogether into Alice's world.

She was the first, last, and only necrophiliac in Wonderland. Or so everyone believes.

MISSION NO 10 COMPLETE.

The blue spong hovered in the hallway, throb, throb, a-throbbing. It then exploded, releasing an orb of azure flames.

The next morning the *Chicago Tribune* headline read:

"CLAMS MANSION BURNED TO THE GROUND."

CPSIA information can be obtained
at www.ICGtesting.com
Printed in the USA
LVOW11s1630270717
542866LV00001B/16/P